# MISTER MALONE

# MISTER MALONE

*for Jordan –*
*"Mister Malone" –*
*Best Always –*
*Weldon*

### by
### Weldon Payne

New Voices Series v. 22

## FAP BOOKS
## FLORIDA ACADEMIC PRESS, INC.
### Gainesville, FL

Published in the United States of America by
Florida Academic Press, Inc. Gainesville, FL, November 2012

Front cover picture designed and by permission of Anibal Rodriguez
Text and cover by David Greenberg Communications, Inc.
Author's photo by permission of Chris Payne


Library of Congress Cataloging-in-Publication Data

Payne, Weldon, 1930-
  Mister Malone / by Weldon Payne.
     pages cm. -- (New voices series ; v. 22)
  ISBN 978-1-890357-39-9
  1. Poor--Fiction. 2. Alabama--Fiction. 3. Domestic fiction. I. Title.
  PS3616.A978M57 2012
  813'.6--dc23
                          2012036360

*For Jill, Scott & Chris who have made their dad wealthy with
rich memories and lasting love.
—Father Fox*

# Prologue

They had come to Ox Hill, Alabama, not by choice but because somebody said a house was empty. They moved in, as though washed on the crest of a swollen river; occupying the empty house not to stay but as another place to store families and old trunks and themselves. It had been a long time since they had chosen anything.

An empty house, and maybe a few leased acres, and close to the mines. They clung to this knowledge just in case some day, by blind chance, their name should turn up on a card—again not by any choice of theirs—and they should as a final rock-bottom refuge be summoned into the bowels of the earth in a last-ditch stand against the thing that had obliterated choosing.

They came without knowing where the two-dollars-a-month rent would come from, without even thinking where it would come from because this would constitute choosing of a sort, and they no longer allowed themselves the luxury of even imagining that they could choose. They took the house (and some the company leases); they could still bet their sweat against the poor, starved, rocky soil, against the cost of Guano, doctor's bills, and fatback.

They moved into the bare-walled houses on cold rainy days as the heavens dumped one last insult on their ragged belongings; occupied old houses with open and sooty flues and rain-streaked walls and barren rooms with faded squares marking where four-legged wood heaters once stood, and if they were lucky maybe a piece or two of usable stovepipe was poked under the floor some place. Else they had to beg, borrow or steal or in some way acquire even that, along with a stove (unless this was among things that had survived, with them, the last move and was lashed on the back of somebody's borrowed truck).

The moving in was private. Smoke, curling on cold wind-less day or lost in wetness signaled an awakening, a stirring inside silent house; smoke leaking new presence of family. Light would flicker again at night in broken windows—wink around striped ticking of torn and stinking feather pillow or old rain-soaked newspaper, cardboard or clothing—lanterns marking the landing of someone else, safe again.

Then on a cold, rainy day, another truck, topped with bed-springs and maybe a few soaked chickens stuck in under rolled-up mattress, would spin into another muddy yard, and another family would unload (alone while eyes watched from kitchen windows) and empty itself into smoked and darkened walls of house.

Windows were never dark for long. Someone always turned up, washed up, without choice, needing refuge for a little while. So they came to Ox Hill.

They came from many different places in that time of national embarrassment and though they were alike in coming without choice, they were different. Each house was a little island, holding whatever privacy they were to have. And this is what was so often misunderstood: On the books they were all alike, these people who came without choice, but they never were.

#

# Chapter 1

Some faint semblance of choice, perhaps, prompted George Malone before he or the woman either had taken a dozen steps after dismounting from the bus to say to her: "I could take one of them a ways for you." (Meaning one of the sacks of groceries that the woman clutched to her so that only her face showed when she turned.)

There was nothing out of the way intended although he smelled her perfume that was like clean-smelling soap, singled out from scent of burning oil, wet pines, and old slag.

He saw her new, while the bus ground out of sight: The two of them separated from noisy strangers and for that moment away from drab, wet, strange old Quarters, and yet in that moment neither of them alone, suddenly not.

Oranges in red netting lay on top of one bag, showing the purple stamp of Color Added. He smelled onions and a faint mustiness and said: "I could carry one for you."

She smiled, hesitated, then relinquished one bag, leaving in view a dark red mark that it had made on the white inside of her arm.

"Well, thank you." Brown eyes cheerful. "It does feel good to move my arm. Again."

Still nothing (careful not to touch), except a slight lifting of spirits for having done some little thing in the old way; yet he was conscious, too, of grimy overalls and sweaty shirt, thinking of these because she had spoken so properly and with a tone that meant she was from somewhere else. And not in the sense that all of them were, but that she had not come from Texas or Arkansas or other parts of Alabama, but perhaps from the North. At any rate she did not belong behind the Quarters, which is where he had seen her go on other days.

Until this day George had never said anything (once or twice nodding), always either waiting until she, with rapid click of heels, moved away, or himself striding ahead so that by the time he reached the turn-off to the Quarters, she was well behind. But it was warm this late afternoon. The ground was starting to dry after fall rains, and he had felt a tiny spark of freedom once he stepped off the stuffy, smoke-choked bus and onto the old paved strip that led to the dirt road and on to Ox Hill.

So he took one of the bags (she insisted that she could manage the other), and they walked together for the brief distance past the Colored house that sat low off the road (and where juke-box lights sparkled from the dark front room and, nights, music and voices reached the road) to where another dirt road with even more mud holes veered to the right past a little store, and on across a black wooden bridge.

Other days, George Malone had seen her walking ahead, fast and small and clean, something in the click of her heels and the movement of her body reminding him of soft-running oiled machinery—turning on that road to the right, dodging holes, walk-ing past the store and other houses where mostly Colored people lived. He had seen her walking alone almost to the bridge on days that he slowed his pace in order to let her get ahead. There was something fresh and orderly about her. Surely she must be afraid, or anxious, in that neighborhood, alone, and he had not wanted to do or say anything that would add to her concern.

But this day he walked with her, conscious of the perfume and of the correctness of her speech, knowing although not dwell-ing on it, that it had made a difference to her, however slight, for him to carry one bag; that she had appreciated it. That it was right. (Not even thinking then that she was pretty; not feeling any particular way about her, although holding in his mind an image of decency from having observed her on the bus, silent in contrast to the loud, slacks-wearing, cigarette-puffing women who also rode the bus.) It was really in appreciation, sort of, that he had wanted to help. As well as whatever it meant to him—a reaching out, a show of concern, a recall from the past when he had worked his own land back in Texas and had helped Tom Scott gather corn. (He had sat through the night with Tom's mother the night she died.) By the simple act today of offering to carry one small bag less than a quarter of a mile, he felt a vague return, or hint anyway, of the possibility for him to be "Mister Malone," a man in position to offer a gesture of help, however small.

Once the word "neighbor" had meant something beyond someone who lived close by, and George had felt a familiarity (late at night with lamp burning in Mrs. Scott's sickroom) stronger than he now felt in his own house. There had been a time when a neighbor would say: "George, I've got this sick cow needs doctoring, and it's too much for one man to manage." Asked openly and without shame or apology, with sureness and ease so unlike the lidded side-long furtive glances here, the indirect, half-whine: "If you wasn't aiming to use that piece a tin I seen laying side of your barn . . ." And unlike the child standing with bare foot raking a naked leg against flies, peering through the screen with a chipped cup in hand, saying softly, not out of courtesy but out of the same fear that kept her father from looking at you: "Mama said did you have some flair . . . ?"

He did not know her name. They talked not about names or where either lived or worked or why they rode the same bus, but about the sunshine and how much rain had fallen and the condition of the roads; until she stopped, a half-step ahead, smiled, saying: "I appreciate this." Brown eyes saying this, too, and nothing more.

So that he walked on, faster, without looking but hearing her quick steps, quieter in the road leading to the bridge, but did not look at her; yet felt vaguely uneasy about a woman like her walking alone past the yellow-painted Colored houses and unpainted gray store and across the black creosoted railroad bridge, and on for what he knew was nearly a half mile, to where the few white families lived next to the woods.

That place, because of the turn of both dirt roads, being not far, but across a hollow from the six and a half company acres, which he plowed and now had planted in cotton (which he and the children and his wife, too, unless her back acted up, would pick if the rain ever stopped long enough).

His uneasy feeling on behalf of the woman was part of the newness, a part of the flick of joy. It was good to find something to be concerned about though he did not think of this. He thought about the cotton as he walked the rest of the way home, and when he hummed, he thought it was because the rains had stopped.

\* \* \*

After that day, they walked together. Some days when Colored people got off the bus, George felt more acutely their being there together. Because the Coloreds were always strangers.

Paula began calling him "Mister Malone" and, although he called her "Miz Hogan," he knew her name was Paula. He knew that she had married Buzz Hogan who was now in the South China Sea and who had brought her there to live, to care for his grandmother while he was away. She had stayed on after the grandmother died. He also knew that she clerked at a store in Willis.

On days when she had bought groceries, George began walking as far as the bridge, never stepping on to it, but carrying the groceries that far and then feeling embarrassed when the time came to hold them out for her to take again, feeling as he would have in burdening a child because she was small although her hands and forearms when she gripped the bags looked strong. He never watched her cross the bridge, but immediately stepped off the road and went down a sloping path to the railroad below.

He could hear her walking on the bridge. From the tracks below, he looked up once and saw celery sticking out of the top of the sack that her small arm encircled tightly. He watched her go bobbling across and out of sight.

On these days, George walked the railroad home, which put him beside the cotton field where he talked with his wife and children before going to the barn for his own cotton sack. He never told at home about helping the woman, or anything about her, not because he had reason to hide anything but because there was no way of telling what it was like. There were times when he wanted to talk about her, what a lady she was and how he felt uneasy about her, not only her walking through the Quarters, but also because she was alone back there, with her husband off sailing somewhere.

* * *

After they had finished the first picking and had started over the field again, it began to get dark early. It was cold when the sun went down. This early dark meant that George had to leave most of the picking to his wife and children, except on Saturdays. It also meant that Paula would soon have to walk home in the dark. George thought of this, while his wife slept. He smelled the old mattresses, musty quilts, the close stuffiness of the closed rooms reeking of boiled cabbage. When a train passed in the night, he thought of how it would go under the bridge, of how Paula might hear it, too, alone in her house behind the Quarters. And be afraid.

Then after quiet returned, he thought of her walking alone after dark, her heels clicking across the bridge, and past Colored men standing in front of the store, and across the bridge. And he would think: Why would a man stick his wife off in a hole like that?

Then he would think of himself and his family and of how far they had come; of the WPA school construction job, which would surely play out by Christmas, and how ashamed he would be if she were to see, to know how his house looked and smelled.

He thought of things he might say to her that were unlike the George Malone he now was; things that she, with her proper way of speaking, would not think strange. He wondered about her house—what it smelled like inside, and he knew that her house would be clean and good-smelling. He hoped that her husband (who had joined the Navy probably because he could not find a job in that godforsaken hole) sent her enough money.

After he had worn himself out thinking (remembering how young she was, and how much it cost him to feed five kids and how his job might not last past Christmas), George would say to himself: I wish Buzz Hogan would come home. Only. Yes. He wished he would come home.

#

# Chapter 2

"That man has been following me," she told him as they walked that evening. Their bus had been late, and the light at the corner of the store was glowing. He glanced ahead, first seeing her young, fresh face and a sprig of honey hair blowing free, then ahead: his glance sweeping the front of the store, trying to see whom she meant. Colored men clustered beside the steps. He looked at them, suddenly afraid for her, but she was speaking softly, saying: "Down by the bridge."

The man who slouched against the railing wasn't Colored although his shadowed face was dark under the black leather cap. He turned his head now to watch them.

George heard Paula's heels on the boards and his own shoes striking wood; walking now, both of them on the bridge. Without turning but peering to the right, George saw the man's eyes white in shadows, his shoulders humped up, saw him spitting over the rail as they passed. Malt, beer scent faint on the wind.

George, carrying two bags of groceries, crossed the bridge in rapid step with her until they were walking on ground again, and she glanced back. He saw her face, her glistening eyes and heard her say quietly, "I'm being silly, Mister Malone."

"No."

"It probably doesn't mean anything."

"Is he still there?"

"Yes. Leaning on the bridge. He has been there three nights. I first saw him last Friday and then again on Monday."

"Does he live back here?"

They were walking on the twisting road, going farther than George had been, away from the houses of the Quarters, between fields. He could see lights between him and the woods, scattered lights from other houses.

"Perhaps he does. Someone new moved into a house back there." She stopped, turned to him. "I'm sorry, Mister Malone. I'll take them now. You need not go all the way."

"I'll tote 'em." (Conscious of the word "tote"—an Ox Hill word. He wished he had said carry.) "How far is it?"

"Just over there. I can take them now."

But George held the bags and moved on and she walked again with him.

"Did he follow you?"

"Yes. He came behind me from the bridge. But it probably didn't mean anything."

A dog was barking as they approached her dark house.

"You be careful."

They were on the porch and she fumbled for the key.

"It's not a safe place for a woman. By yourself." He was looking back up the road and listening, but it was quiet except for the dog. Then the door was open and light came on inside. She stood in the doorway, holding the screen open with her body.

The inside of her house smelled like soap—clean and sharp—and instantly he saw a picture of the dark eyes—younger—on the mantel, and the sailor. Cheeks touching.

She gestured to the table because George hadn't given up the groceries but had entered, unasked. Neither of them said anything until finally she had relieved him of the bags and placed them on the neat table, having picked up something, rearranged something.

A small naked bulb dangled from the ceiling. White thin

curtains shielding the yellow window-shade while George turned, under the light, toward the open door, and she said, "I've made you late."

"That don't—doesn't—matter." He half-turned, stopped to look at her. "It's not safe, back here by yourself."

"I get so . . ." Her lips seemed stiff, her face tight. "So lonesome." Tears brimmed. There was the color of honey in her hair. And he noticed a tiny scar to the left of her mouth.

"If I was you," he said, "I'd go back home."

"I can't."

They stood near the dangling bulb, which was not much higher than his head. "You can't stay here. Stuck off by yourself."

"You are good to worry," she said softly. Her lips were not moving properly; her voice was unsteady. "You are so kind."

George back-stepped and, feeling behind him, opened the screen. He cleared his throat. "You lock your doors good, hear?"

She nodded, but he wasn't sure she had heard: Her eyes said she had not.

Then she was there, in front of him, small yet so large he saw nothing else. He felt her hand, light on his arm, and smelled perfume. Her voice, small, was saying, "Be careful." Her eyes, in that instant, were huge, soft, and George felt his arms trying to move. "Go back home!" he blurted.

He saw light in her hair and knew she was closing the door. He wanted to stop it, to hold that second against darkness.

Into the cold night and on to the little dirt road, away from that clean-smelling house while the dog barked and the sweet smell of her blocked the cold air, George almost did not see what suddenly was no longer shadow but now hulking body and hidden face under dark leather cap beside the ditch; hard face materializing, grin sure and certain not five feet away; shadowed grinning face that would haunt sleepless nights.

George walked quickly, without looking back, toward the light atop a pole at the store—cold hollow goneness inside his stomach. Going finally across the bridge and turning, sliding, down to the tracks until he was where the light could not reach, and at last stepped on to the broken boards of his own porch and went inside, to the kitchen where his wife, without looking from the stove, said: "What kept you?"

#

# Chapter 3

George watched the red bus lights disappear, felt blackness suck in, envelop him. He had a sensation of being in the vast black sky rather than on the ground. He looked toward where the bus had disappeared. Cold windless night bit his nostrils. He moved, finally, crunching gravel.

She could have told me. Didn't have to up and leave without a word.

He walked fast, casting no shadow. If she did leave. Is gone. Like noise from the bus. Like glow from its lights. He looked behind, as though another bus might have appeared; stopped, listened, then walked again. Slower. I told her to. I said go home. But I didn't . . .

Then he was at the road—her road. He wanted to take it, to cross the bridge to see if she had indeed gone. Maybe she just missed the bus. Or maybe . . . Suddenly it was fear, not anger; maybe that guy had broken in on her. He imagined her struggling, helpless.

George stood at the crossroads. All day he had thought about her and waited to see her, to be assured that nothing had happened; that what most of the night he had worried about might happen had not. He stepped on to her road.

Go home. Forget it and go home. Forget her. All right.

He was going home now, but he could no more forget— that creep, her vulnerability, George's own helplessness to even know—than he could forget that moment in her doorway. Or sweet perfume or brown eyes and honey hair or tone of her saying: Mister Malone.

Nor could he forget, at midnight with the old familiar smells surrounding him—lived-in, slept-in, wood-smoked house—her, whom he hardly knew.

*  *  *

It rained on Saturday as George sat with two of his older children in the crib, shucking corn. Rain, blowing, peppered the roof, swept softly against the warped planks. In the dark and musty quiet, George smelled the cold rain. Maybe she is sick. Maybe she thinks I don't care. Maybe . . . it slipped in like a knife . . . *maybe*. Filthy pig. Smashing door. I don't really know her. So lonesome back there. She touched my arm. I felt . . .

She did not mean anything. Did she? (George saw the ugly grin under billed cap.) What if he has been there, was still there . . . who would have heard her scream? Rain pelting roof now.

"What's the matter, Daddy?" asked Nathan.

"Nothing." I at any rate cannot do anything and I might as well forget her. I just want, wanted

Mister Malone. Mister Malone.

He thought of her perfume and of how he had wanted to touch her hair. She ought to go away. Maybe she has already gone. But I hope she is all right.

"You want us to feed this to the mule, Daddy?"

"Yeah, Son. Then y'all scoot on to the house."

Dampness swept in through the opened door, and the noise of rain grew louder. Willa Marie squealed and scrunched in the doorway a second before darting out into the rain. "It's cold," she cried as the door scraped against the ground and closed. George heard his daughter's voice, faint, moving away.

I just want her to be all right and for him not to ever bother

her. I would not defile her. I would not do anything . . .

He righted a bucket, which had been turned on its side. The barn is old, run down and ratty, and water is leaking now in that corner. He watched the dripping water splatter on an empty corn shuck. He felt in his overalls bib for a quarter-plug of Big Apple; cut a corner and slipped it into his mouth.

I don't know what I want except it was where we could walk together and I could talk with her and there was nothing wrong with that, with how it has been because there is nobody on this godforsaken hill that I mean a pee in the bucket to or that I can give anything to and what if he did actually break in on her?

In that moment when she looked at me straight her eyes were not like the way they are when she talks. They were bigger but not only that, there was no strangeness even though the face was different, like I had not seen it before, and that is when I thought of kissing when I felt I had known her forever.

George spat into the shadows. Dummy! You're just a nice old coot to her . . . *So kind* . . . In the midst of the musty, dusty corncob dank and ratty smell, mixed in the damp falling winter-coming rain scent and sharp chewing-tobacco twang, though not mixed but superior to all of these and rising above and alone in the dimness came her sweet perfume, clear and strong. He sat very still, afraid to move lest he upset the delicate moment. If I could just talk to her. See her.

There was a tugging at the door. He heard the uneven boards clutch the ground, saw wide boards moving, saw little fingers gripping inside. Gray lightness broke through as Willa Marie snatched the door open. "Mama says we need some flair, Daddy."

"Flour. It's flour, Honey. They don't say 'flair' in Texas."

"She says we need some. And some cough syrup for Ralphie."

"All right. I'll go to the Quarters to the store in a little bit."

"Can I go?"

"I 'spect not, Honey. It's nasty out."

She stood in the doorway, looking at him. Her dress had been made from feed sacks: purple flowers on white. She wore a red sweater unbuttoned. Her legs looked small in the white socks bunched above scuffed shoes.

"Come in," George said. "Out of the rain." He held out his hand and Willa Marie went to him. He hugged her. "Are you warm enough?"

"Yeah."

"Your hair is wet." She snuggled and he stroked the brown strands of hair clinging to her face.

"Is it all right if we go to Sunday school tomorrow? If it quits raining. Mister Sanders said we could ride in the back of his truck."

"Maybe so, Hon. We'll see. Run along now. Tell your mama I'll go to the store in a little while."

#

# Chapter 4

Red clay bank ahead where the tracks curved, turning toward and then under the bridge past the Quarters toward the mines. Sprinkling rain. Dark gray slag soaked from the heavier chilling showers that had continued into early afternoon. Coal dust streaked the crossties.

George walked between the rails, stepping wide to touch the cracked and creosoted ties. Brown rusty spikes stuck an inch or so above metal plates. Broken bottles, twisted metal bands, curled barbed wire lay between the rails.

It was cold, and as he entered the place between the high red banks, a wind was rising. He smelled wet pines from the hill, dank rotting leaves. He turned up the collar of his blue-checked mackinaw. He would not let himself think beyond the bridge although he knew he would go to her house.

As wind, blowing down the long stretch of railroad, whipped his face, he knew there was something building: an eagerness as he saw the rails come together in a narrow point up ahead, and, before this, black wooden bridge a half-mile away. He dabbed at his leaking nose. He felt strong, alive, with a warm urgency inside him like a buried live coal.

He thought: what if her husband has come home? Maybe this is why she was not on the bus yesterday. Maybe I can't see her after all. I might be able to tell by looking at the house whether she is gone or if she is all right.

The path up the bank was slippery, and the knee of his overalls picked up red smudge when his foot slipped. A kid from one of the Colored houses was sitting on a bicycle, middle of the bridge, leaning over the rail to watch George scale the steep bank. Sullenly he watched as George stepped on to the thick planks.

"Mistuh, you got a quatah?"

"Afraid not," said George as he walked on.

"Bet you is."

He followed the road, sidestepping mud holes. Ice by midnight. An abandoned Chevrolet hood, bedsprings, stove wood piled on porch of tar-papered shanty. He was aware of a stunted, black calf, hair matted, beside the road. Shaggy curs snarled from the yards. Seeing everywhere a barren desolation, but not seeing, either, until at last he did see, on the left at the edge of a brittle-weed-thick field, her house: Brown paint fading, tin roof and, from a chimney on the far side, blue smoke drifting, thinning out against gray sunless sky.

He was aware of other houses, but he did not count them. Any more than later he could have said whether the tree in her yard was oak or chinaberry because the smoking chimney buoyed his hope of seeing her. And if a sailor was inside—he slowed his gait, paused for one tick of a second thinking they might this moment be in bed—then, well, he would think of something.

George touched the crease of his gray felt hat, tugging the brim slightly to tilt over his right eye. He hated the stubble on his face.

The door knob was white, the kind his wife once used as a nest-egg, and he knew exactly how it would feel—hard cold solid—though he did not touch it. Aware of a slope underfoot, George knocked lightly, his breathing suspended in that instant of commitment. He stepped back, seeing, in that stopped second, clothes on a line and wondered, on a day like this **why**. He was reaching to knock again when the door opened.

The face was at first only a face, then focused pieces coming together, falling into place 'til yes, it was the face remembered, the dreamed-of same face.

"Mister Malone!" Her hand touched her mouth, then the kerchief, which hid the hair except for a curl that fell like a broken spring on to her forehead. Her hands were smoothing the sides of the men's pants she wore; her hand caught the tail of a loose, too-big chambray shirt and made a move toward the thin belted waist. She smiled.

"Are you all right?" He scraped his shoes on the planks and stepped inside, clutching his hat with both hands.

Her hand touched her face again. "I can't believe . . ."

"Well, I was afraid, maybe, you might be sick . . ."

"I'm fine. I'm sorry I look so horrible. This (hands spreading, settling lightly over both breasts) is Buzz's shirt. And these old pants . . ."

"I had to come to the store, anyway. I been worried."

She smiled as though remembering some secret, happy thing. "Sit down. Sit back here at the table, and I'll get some coffee. It won't take a minute."

Her house fit closely around George, walls snugly enclosing. Singing inside his head: I am inside her house. With her.

"I was worried about that guy. I passed him the other night. He didn't bother you, I reckon?"

"No! I shouldn't have told you about him. It was silly."

"You can't ever tell."

She moved so he could see her, turned toward him while her hands were busy with the coffee. He saw the high cheekbones and smooth throat curving from the faded blue collar.

"After you left I thought I heard someone on the porch, but I guess it was a dog, or maybe I was hearing things."

"You got a gun?"

"No," she said and laughed. "I wouldn't know what to do with a gun."

"I was uneasy about you. He was standing beside the road right out there when I left."

She brought the coffee. She had removed the kerchief. "It's nice of you to worry about me."

"You don't know how I hated to go with him hanging around."

She sat across from George. "I wish I had something . . . oh, I know." She darted into the kitchen and returned with doughnuts.

"Miz Hogan . . ."

"Paula."

"All right. You call me George, then."

Her shiny eyes looked happy. "I'll try," she said.

"I didn't mean to meddle when I said you ought to go home. But I can't help worrying about you." He swallowed hot coffee, careful to do it quietly.

"You're good to me." She raised her cup, drank without looking at him.

"I just . . ." He cleared his throat. "It means something to me, the way it's been. To know you, I mean. Since we moved here, seems like I'm amongst strangers. But not like that with you."

"I know."

He stood. "I reckon you do. I'm going to have to go. My boy's sick."

She stood, too, and her hands played with the back of a chair. Her eyes were bright when she turned away.

"Aw, look." George went to her. Gently he touched her arms. She turned; his hands helped her turn. He drew her close.

Her eyes widened, and he thought in that split-second that he had made a terrible mistake. Then she was against him. His face felt her soft hair. Her head pushed against him, turning, struggling for freedom so that her face could, did, come around and was, then, in the right place, accessible.

In that sure fraction of a second—that sensuous, intimate,

irrevocable and inevitable dot of time before he kissed her—he knew things would never be the same. Just before their lips met she drew in her breath, but she met him as he kissed her; her lips not small at all, not prim, fragile, untouchable, but soft warm yielding.

George's hands fell away as though of their own accord, but she held him, slipping her hands in under his arms, hugging him through the bulky jacket. Her face lay against him.

"I won't ever quit worrying, late at night, over here by yourself." He pulled away. "I've got to go."

She took his hand.

"I got to," he said.

A moment later he stumbled on the steps, then made his way across the yard to the pocked dirt road leading to the bridge. His brogans splashed through a mud puddle. He heard a yearling bawl somewhere.

#

# Chapter 5

It was, he knew, a dangerous and bottomless happiness. Even as he slid down the bank and walked the tracks toward home, there was the start of a new worry. His uneasiness about her would be worse now. Already forming was concern about his inability to fulfill what, to his way of thinking, was some kind of commitment.

dead barren fields and cluttered yards and the gray which almost always hovered over him—gone

He thought of that moment when he had known positively that he was about to kiss her; that she willed it.

His head was filled with the spring-flower scent of her and with the fresh touch of her mouth in that second after the quick intake of breath. And that other—that certain and sure and almost-forgotten feel of about-to-touch yielding flesh when her face turned toward his. And the quick rise of desire returned, lingered like her scent, surged.

Wintry sky was darkening when he rounded the curve between the high banks. He felt a sadness, with night coming. The kiss—that moment of certainty when she struggled to free her face for him—this kiss blotting out a helpless feeling that had been with him for a long time although he did not fully realize this enough to recognize it. He hummed without knowing it as he watched patches of grape clouds stretching in the cold sky where the sun should have been.

Nor did he know, on that November evening with night fast coming, what he would do next; what, if anything, lay beyond the commitment of that kiss.

Moving away from that moment, away from her (he no longer could look over his shoulder and see the bridge that led to her house) he saw, past the big willow in their cow lot, the back side of his barn, and hunched-up sweater caught his eye—his wife, milking in cold twilight. *Oh god.*

The Jersey cow, old-sooty tan hide blending, almost lost in shadows in that alcove, faced the feed trough. George felt the ache, then, the lonely grip and stir; a familiar scene returning, knowing even before he could make out the movement of her elbows as she tugged at the teats, how her lips would be pursed, making a soft whistling sound. Thelma, familiar, bringing the barn into focus and the house beyond and the old picture of how it had been, *how it was now.*

Leaving the railroad, George stooped to squeeze between two strands of barbed wire. He followed a path through the pasture, past the willow, past the sour pig-pen smell, and saw before he had taken two steps, a car pulling into the yard on the other side of the railroad from his barn. The car pulled a rubber-tired cart loaded with coal.

He was close enough to hear milk cutting through foam into the pail that Thelma held between her knees, before she turned.

"High time you got back. Thought I'd have to send the sheriff after you. Ralphie's coughing his head off."

"I got him some syrup. You want to go on to the house, I'll finish."

"No need now. It's pert near dark. I couldn't wait forever."

George looked at her dark tousled hair; saw her broad rump in the faded print dress spread on an upturned bucket. "I see the Gordons have stole themselves another load of coal," he said.

"That's no concern of mine. If the railroad people don't

have better sense than to park a loaded car out in the middle of nowhere, what else can they expect? Give me that syrup, I've got to see about the baby. You can bring the flour on, I reckon."

She walked away. The Jersey was licking hard to get the yellow powdered feed from the corners of the trough. George heard the rough tongue against wood. He untied the halter rope and led the cow to the stall, slapped her flank and turned the wood latch.

He stood, not thinking about anything, looking at the chicken house. The pen was empty; hens and roosters would be perched inside on their roosts. He heard the mule wrestling an ear of corn; great teeth chomping.

George felt the ache again beyond the bridge and Paula neat clean lonely probably at that moment cooking supper. While he could not reconcile this to the scene around him, he was feeling a way he had not felt in a long time. Without any choosing, he thought of her now and smelled again the scent of spring flowers as he walked toward the old paintless house.

#

# Chapter 6

Sometime during the night, while he was dreaming of a wheat field in west Texas, Thelma awakened George.

in his dream she had come with his lunch a bright sun blinding

Slowly he realized it was not sunlight but fire from a wick glowing inside a sooty globe held close.

"Ralphie's burning up with fever. You're gonna have to get a doctor."

Thelma's bosom sagged inside the feed-sack gown, her eyes hollow in lamp's glare. George, fighting to come out of the black sleep-mines, smelled coal-oil.

"Is he sick?" Not yet awake, but enough to know it was not a good question.

"I told you he's burning up. Choked up in his lungs. You better get a doctor."

Then he saw, on the cot across the room, Ralphie's chest rising and falling in too quick jerks. "I don't know where to get a doctor." He was on his feet, reaching for overalls. "Closest phone, I guess, is the Glovers."

"Why don't you try to get one from Blackwater?"

I ought to have known better that moment coming back now but without joy or passion fear flashing across the years to a night when he had sat with the Jimson boy; the night he died with pneumonia.

"It'd be closer," he said. "The thing is, whether they'd come. They're company doctors."

"Surely to goodness they'd come if you paid first. There's money in the trunk."

"Depends on which one and what kind of notion he's in." George held Ralphie's wrist, counting the rapid pulse the way a Texas doctor had taught him. "I'll try it. Else I'll have to call Marbletown, and Lord knows when he'd get here from there."

"Tell them he's burning up . . ."

"Daddy's going to get the doctor-man for you," George told Ralphie. "Make you better." He laid a hand on Ralphie's head and looked at Thelma. "I'll be back soon's I can."

"The lantern's in the kitchen," she said, stuffing four bills into his pocket.

There was ice, thin, at the edge of the field where he entered the woods finding, with lantern's glow, washed-out path that led downhill to the mining camp. Even then, even with woods close around him, surrounded by shadows, feeling himself pushed, moving not so much at his own will but moving, not even knowing if he could get a doctor, even then George thought of her. Wished she could know what was happening. Thinking of her, he was aware of a small glow—different, without urgent desire, but a good unexplainable feeling a knowing and a need to tell her about his sick boy.

A light was shining inside the clinic, close to the redbrick commissary, but George had to knock several times before, finally, a tall, slightly stoop-shouldered man came into view, fumbled with the door, opened it slightly. "What is it?" (The voice alone gouging George, even without the hard-brown squinting eyes or tilt of the head.)

"Doctor, my boy's sick. Burning up with fever, and I was wondering if maybe you could come . . ."

"Where do you live?" (A huge hand had found rimless glasses, quickly placed them above the bony nose.)

"Up on the hill."

"Ox Hill?" (The hand rubbed the chin. Eyes studied George.) "You work in the mines?"

"No I don't, doctor. But my boy's sick. I can pay. I've got the money here." George's hand fumbled with the wrinkled bills.

"You not employed by the company?"

"I work on a project. But I can pay . . . I'm afraid it's pneumonia."

It was cold where George stood, and he thought of asking if he might step inside, but no. He would not do that. He would get on his knees to get Ralphie a doctor, but it was all right about the cold. It was better about that than the cold in the doctor's eyes.

"Well, see, what's your name?"

"Malone. George Malone."

"Well, you see, Malone, we're not supposed to treat anybody excepting employees of the company. And their families. Is the boy wheezing?"

"You can hear him across the room," said George. He could hear his own voice as though it were not his, saying, "I was just afraid it might be pneumonia."

"Mmm-huh. You say you work on a project? You mean one of Mister Roosevelt's projects?"

"I reckon so, yes. If you mean WPA. Doctor, here's four dollars. If that's not enough . . ."

"Oh. Oh, no, it's not the money. It's just policy. Let me see." He studied his watch. "I think maybe what we ought to do is to—it's quarter after midnight. I can call you a doctor out of Marbletown. I'll . . ." He seemed to still be half asleep, but he turned, started toward the back, remembered. "Why don't you step in out of the cold? I'll see if I can get Dr. Cunningham. You say he's wheezing?"

"He's all clogged up. I'd appreciate it if you could get some help for him."

"Yes. Well. Why don't you come in?"

Wishing later that he had done what once he would have, only back then would not have needed to, wishing he had stayed where he was: That's all right, Mister Doctor, I wouldn't come into your office personally if it was forty below. Wishing this, but actually going inside, following as the old man fumbled with a telephone.

(Smelling medicine, George did not enjoy or appreciate it as he had in the past in doctors' offices—that smell always before had nudged him, touching a faint and buried urge; touching the same part of him that was affected when, then, he had doctored a sick horse or sewed up a ruptured hog, but now he would not allow himself any of this.)

Once he was outside again and felt the cold in his nostrils, walking across the flat place toward the hill and the woods and home again, having been told that Cunningham would be out in a little while (driving from Marbletown) George thought (still smelling the sharp sickly odors): What if *she* got sick in the middle of the night?

Stars were out now, and he could see the white lining of dark clouds floating in an almost moonless sky. Light flowed in all directions from his lantern and, on the cold night air, the sulfuric rotten-egg scent from the mines was powerful.

I could not help her. I would not even know. Even if I knew I could not help her. He was still angry about the doctor and only slightly relieved about Ralphie; knowing anyway that he had done all he could do, although this knowledge, rather than comforting, was part of the deeper hollow worry, the helpless knowing that he could do so little, and nothing now except wait; that whatever had taken control had got him out of bed to beg for a chance to spend his money so his boy might not die; had brought him to the point that the nails he drove with special pride and as much care as always, and the boards he still carefully squared were somehow tainted by three initials, which people like the squint-eyed doctor resented (mainly as a symbol of a deeper hatred for a cripple named Roosevelt), all of this standing between him and his ability to do what any man ought to be able to do—help his child in time of sickness.

In the midst of his hollowness, even though he tried not to think about it or to let it happen (because he knew it was even worse to do so under the circumstances); nevertheless, there came a clear image of Paula: Curled up in bed, alone on the other side of the Quarters while that guy with the leather-billed cap low over his ears maybe lurked on her porch.

George felt a wave of caring which, even with Ralphie sick and even remembering what, a few hours ago, had happened in her house, was free of guilt; although not free of pain and not totally of pride because George thought, knew under the darkening sky, that she, having in that special moment accepted him, was now a part, maybe like family, of his concern and worry.

Entering the narrow path between the first cluster of trees, he felt again, in spite of himself, a lifting, on some level, of his spirit.

#

# Chapter 7

It was, after all, not planned except for the thousand and one scenes sketched in his mind night and day from the time he first held her, from that slow moment when she had first turned her face upward and warm yielding face, lips, found his.

But George missed the bus at the school site, through no fault of his but because Henry McIntosh decided at five minutes before quitting time to discuss prospects of their future employment; saying how, even allowing for bad weather, the school job would be finished no later than the first of January, after which it did not look promising; chose this moment "just on account of I wanted to give you men as much notice as I could with Christmas coming on."

The news, which really was not news but confirmation of what George already knew, nevertheless hit him coldly in the stomach; even so not hitting as hard as the realization, when he got to his stop and saw the rear of the bus he had meant to catch rounding a curve, and thought I won't see her tonight.

Plus the fact that a mist, threatening all day, was beginning to fall, and he started walking, in response to whatever it was that pushed him from day to day. Walking away from the pale light, which showed vacant school yard and closed-up front of Shepherd's Grocery. Light speckled glass top of a gas pump half-filled with 19-cent-a-gallon fuel, which he wished he needed.

Empty, more or less numb after Henry McIntosh's announcement, accepting this latest decision from whatever outside source—whatever nameless WPA administrator or maybe something else—which had had hold of him for longer than he cared to remember, George turned, half-heartedly raising his hand as lights came from behind, unevenly cutting through the blackness. Before it slowed, came abreast and went past, finally stopping after cutting to the grassy side, he knew it was a truck, although he did not notice the lumber piled haphazardly on the short bed until it had stopped.

"Where y'all going?" the driver asked when George approached and wrestled the door open.

"Ox Hill."

It was maybe a half mile farther on, while rain speckled the cracked windshield and the driver had informed him (rolling the window down and spitting) that "It's about to turn cold," that George first thought, then knew, what he would do.

"You want some goobers, there's some in that sack."

"No. Much obliged."

Knowing (and without realizing it, choosing, and in that moment feeling relief) that he would see Paula, though even then not allowing himself to think beyond this. The thought itself was the best thing that had happened all day. It blotted out McIntosh's words, and for a while erased the worry—which George had never gotten around to articulating—as to what he would do after the first of January.

"I'll get out right down here."

"If I can get this thing stopped. Frazzling brakes about gone."

"What do I owe you?"

"Nothing. I got a certain ways to go no matter who's with me. You better take some of the goobers."

"Much obliged to you for the ride."

George saw bits of water glistening in the light in front of the store. The bridge was wet, but he paid little attention to anything until, down the road, he saw the yellow glow that meant she was home. Knowing his knock would frighten her, but knocking anyway, he said, "Paula?"

The light went out.

"It's Malone."

The door opened slightly, then wider, and the screen came toward him, and she was there on the shadowed porch, close.

"What happened? I wondered about you?"

"Shhh."

Inside, his eyes sought her in the darkness; her face, close, slowly coming into focus. "The switch is there, somewhere . . ." But he stopped her and held her where she was. Her scent was lustrous enough as he gathered her to him, his hands burying into her hair, feeling through the softness, bringing his rough palms around to the side, lifting her face.

It was raining harder. They heard it on the tin roof.

"Lord, I've thought about you. Is it . . ."

She kissed away the question. She was on her toes (shorter, because she was barefoot. He liked this). He held her there, lifted. He was aware of how she stretched, came up on her toes, which put her thighs hard against his while his arms held her, lifting even more.

"You're wet," she whispered against his face. Her hands slipped inside his jacket, snuggled into the sleeves, worming their way close to the hard upper-arm muscles. (Her mouth was so much stronger than it looked.)

"Here, let me . . ." He shucked off the jacket. Her hand slid inside the bib of his overalls, moving against his body. Her tiny trembling noises floated to the surface.

Rain rippled across the tin roof, blown like bird-shot by a rising wind, and whatever words were spoken, if any, he would not remember. A door creaked; he felt a draft from another room, which they entered.

Darkness changed slightly, or his eyes adjusted so that after he had bumped the bed, the dim white spread materialized and she was free from him, darkness within darkness, sitting on the bed. He heard the whisper of sheet; saw the separate shadow moving; heard, saw the faint sinking of petite shadow onto dim white, stretching out there; lifting, her hands busy with something that dropped lightly to the floor. Moving into that suspended moment, his knee buried, sank into the mattress, only then saying "Wait." "Wait."

He moved beside her, approaching; aware then of overalls—rushed, awkward, and clumsy—and of heavy brogans, thinking: I must not get mud on her bed. Saying: "I . . ."

She touched his face.

His hand found her, even then not believing, suddenly he was unable to believe.

Waiting, aware of having to wait, realizing it but moving as though there was nothing to wait for; puzzled, sinking feeling hitting home. "I . . ."

Raising on his elbow, fumbling, verifying, but still vainly pushing, unfeeling, retreating.

She waited. In that sinking eternity, he knew she waited.

"Something's wrong," he whispered. "I don't . . ."

She was still.

"I can't. I . . ."

"Shhh."

In that lost black moment, even before turning away, sitting again with both feet on the floor, the hurt was for her. "I don't know what happened. I just . . . can't."

"It's all right." Her breath was close to his ear, arms around him.

He slapped his leg. "It's not all right! I'm sorry."

"You're tired."

"I'm not." He heard the rain. And the hollow buzz of quiet.

"I wanted . . ." he said when he was on his feet, moving,

pushed by whatever it was, blindly away.

He heard the springs as she moved behind him. He heard her bare feet on the floor and felt her arms, her head somewhere against his back. As he started through the door, a whisper.

# Chapter 8

He ate the steaming white beans and the cornbread that Thelma had kept warm, washing them down with buttermilk and hot coffee.

"I was afraid some bum had knocked you in the head."

George stared at the oil-cloth, aware of the lamp in the center of the table, seeing the half-filled level of the coal-oil, aware, too, of the kids, clustered in the kitchen.

"You ought to get some dry clothes on."

George shrugged. He did not tell about the job. He might not tell. That was not the important thing. He could not think of the important thing. Paula. He did not have to think of her or of what had happened any more than he had to think of the wet clothes.

"We got another scare," said Thelma. "Right after dark. The girls and me had to go out. Down the hill, there, in the back. We were waiting on Mary Sue. Willa Marie heard it first."

"Heard what?"

"Somebody out there. Or something. We heard it moving down below us, around the empty coops."

"A dog or something?"

"Wasn't no dog!" said Willa Marie.

"Too big for a dog," said Thelma. "I couldn't see anything. Black as pitch, and it had started raining."

"What'd it sound like? Maybe somebody's stock got loose."

"Sounded like somebody."

"I heard him," Willa Marie said. "Somebody walking slow. I heard him step on a stick."

"Jack had been barking," Thelma said. "I heard him barking earlier, off toward the barn."

"I got the shotgun," Nathan said. "I was going out there, but Mama wouldn't let me."

"Maybe y'all was just hearing things. Raining and all. You didn't actually see anything, did you?"

"I thought I did," said Willa Marie. "I thought I saw something moving down there."

"We didn't stick around to investigate," his wife said. "We got ourselves in the house fast as we could. It wasn't rain. I felt like somebody was watching us, even before Willa Marie said anything."

"Didn't Jack bark then? Where was Jack?"

"Maybe he knocked Jack in the head," said Nathan.

"Nah," Sammy said. "Jack would have bit him."

"Looks like he might have barked."

"Probably off rambling," Thelma said. "It wasn't fifteen, twenty minutes before, he was barking up a storm out the barn."

"Quit going outside after dark!" George snapped. He gulped coffee and sat with fists knotted on the oil-cloth.

"Well, what do you expect us to do, then?"

"Use the slop-jar."

"It was so early," she said. She began moving things on the stove. "Y'all go on and get ready for bed."

"Did you tell him about the cow, Mama?"

"What about the cow? Say?"

"Nothing," his wife said. "Some yahoo wanted to buy her. This afternoon. Nathan talked to him."

"Who? I don't reckon our cow's for sale. Yet. Who was it?"

"I was slopping the hogs, Daddy, and this guy, I never seen him before, came around the corner. I looked up and he was standing there, looking at me, and I asked what he wanted. Said: 'You wanta sell that cow?' I told him I didn't reckon, that he'd have to see you. He asked who you was and said he reckon he might know you. Then he walked off down the railroad."

"What'd he look like?"

"Kinda big and dark like."

"Had on a leather cap," Thelma said. "I was going out to milk and saw him when he walked off and got back on the railroad."

"It was down over his eyes," said Nathan. "He looked funny, like maybe it was too big for his head."

"He said he knew me?"

"Said he might."

"Go on to bed," George said. "Nate, anybody comes poking around, you tell him to see me, you hear?"

"If it's not one aggravation around this dump, it's two," said Thelma. She sat down on the bench across the table. It was, George thought, as though they were in a storm cellar—tight and unreal.

"I never felt so helpless, George. Stuck off like this."

"I can't help it." Lord, don't start that.

"Didn't say you could." She was looking down at her twisting hands. "Don't reckon anybody can. Least we had neighbors in Horton."

George took a deep breath. Horton, and the way it had been there—how he had been—was as far gone as the way Thelma had once been. He wanted her to look at him.

"We may not be here much longer, anyhow," he said. "Job's playing out first of the year."

He saw her knuckles whiten and watched her grip the table. He saw, too, the stranger's eyes, angry as they looked at him.

"That's what McIntosh had to tell, how come I missed the bus."

"Well, what do you aim to do?"

Why are you asking me? For the question, coming from a

woman who had once looked up to him as though he were capable of doing anything, was empty because the only thing he knew at that moment was that unless whatever it was in control of his life intervened, he was going to bed as quickly as possible. Though he did not think that he would sleep. Flat on his back now, vision of small shadow on dim white and whisper of silk and that moment—that petrifying moment when he had realized that he could not give, couldn't even accept what he would never forget being offered.

Smelling the spring flowers and smoky wood coals from the heater, also hearing her soft whispers and remembering, as though it were still in his hand, the touch of her thigh where he had clasped last before abandoning what had left him already.

If I could talk to her, if I could tell her, if I could . . . oh now I could!

Awake long after he heard Thelma's heavy breathing, keeping vigil to the unslumbering desire, George felt breakable. Fragile inside, for she was not just a woman caught in a feverish passion. She was Paula—good, clean, sweet-smelling and proper—Paula who loved him and was a lady. She said you're just tired.

I can't even do wrong *right*. Remembering, too, in that moment of approach not believing that it was about to happen and thinking, knowing that he could not, must not, impregnate her. Even stronger was a fixed image of her innocence, perhaps rooted in her calling him Mister Malone—of what she had at first thought of him. Did she still think of him as Mister Malone? She will probably not want to see me again.

I kept thinking, somewhere thinking: that I must not. What have I done to her anyway, and how does she feel. Now?

Wind whipped a sash of water against the house, against the windowpanes, and he thought of the bird-shot rain on her tin roof, thought of her alone, and wanted to scream in the dark: Paula!

#

# Chapter 9

That morning, the very idea that there could any longer be such a thing as privacy pertaining to him or his, was in itself a shock. Yet it was this invasion of privacy even more than anger and loss that swept over George when Sammy came to the house as he was drinking a second cup of coffee and told him, "Somebody stole the runt."

Examining the pen, re-nailing a rough board that had been knocked loose and following a little way the trail of footprints and marks made by a dragged sack, George knew that, yes, his privacy had been violated.

Some stranger had come into that forsaken place that he loosely and erroneously referred to as his and (with violence to what really was his because he had built the pen) had stolen the only shoat that a man could easily carry away—the black runt from the red sow's spring litter.

"Maybe it was the Gordons," Nathan suggested. "They steal coal."

"I don't think so." Without looking toward the railroad, without looking anywhere other than staring at the V-shaped, dish-water-slop-stained trough while biting a chew of tobacco, George thought: I know who it was.

Which, assuming he was right, meant that the man who had stolen his pig was the man with the leather cap who was lurking near the empty coops while his wife and daughters were outside.

"What're you going to do, Daddy?"

Why are you asking me? He looked at the rough planks and rusty wire, at mud-titted sow, at the muddy male twin-clumps of the sprawled black boar, scenting the sour, rancid air.

What do you do when you cannot put a lock on or stand with shotgun every hour or chain your wife and daughters to their beds, or trust the goodness and sanctity of "neighbor" when you don't even own the land you occupy, which you did not even so much as choose (except by the greatest stretch of the imagination); what do you do against the cold grinning dark face (who also more than likely has been peeping in *her* window) and now has followed you here, figured it out?

What do you do to keep anything of value safe from someone who would not even understand the meaning of "mine?"

(Any more than you could, while riding a ship somewhere on the other side of the world, protect your wife, keep her from lying down in darkness with one who has never stolen anything from any neighbor. Before.)

"I bet that's how come Jack was barking so much," Sammy said. "I bet ole Jack tried to bite his leg off."

"Where is Jack?" Turning slowly. "Nate, you seen Jack this morning?"

Even while the boys called and whistled, and George looked up the slope, he knew that the familiar, lop-eared, no-'count dog could not be protected either. And so he was not surprised to see a few minutes later, close to the big willow, the hound lying with his front legs crossed, neck twisted and eyes frozen, not reflecting anything—a gash no longer red but dried black, a six-inch smear where the collar should have been.

"Get the shovel," he said, when the boys, having seen him stop between the willow and the railroad, had come up quietly; still quiet, save for Sammy's sobs.

"He come over here to die," Nathan said.

"Yes." Remembering and knowing then what that other

smear on the knocked-out board of the pen was; having seen it but thought it was from the thief, not the beloved and useless Jack; thinking that whoever had stolen the runt had gouged himself on a bent nail or wire barb and might, just might, get lockjaw.

Though I reckon, he thought, as he scooped out the shallow hole on the slope above the pen, I reckon Buzz Hogan did not have to be home for his wife to be, technically, safe.

"Can we get another dog?"

George patted the grave with the flat of the spade.

"Huh, Daddy?"

If he would cut a dog's throat what else might he do? To her?

"Say, Daddy? Can we get another dog?"

"Just hush about it," Nathan said.

Or to them. That's who I ought to think about. Them. To where it's not even safe for them to go outside to crap on the hillside.

"I saw a pleece shepherd between here and school that's going to have pups," Sammy said. "Could we get one of them, Daddy? Or maybe we could get her, then if anybody tried to . . ."

"Shut up, Sammy!" He threw the spade, like a spear, downhill. "Y'all get to the house. See what your mama's got needs doing. There's plenty of wood to cut if you got nothing to do. Go on!"

He saw the boys passing the barn, Nathan with an arm around the little one.

"Grunt, damn you!" George said. Because the sow (not the red one, but her daughter, Gussie, being fattened for slaughter in a separate portion of the pen) was grunting loudly, something having disturbed her slumber. George looked at the pink snout pressed against the pen; saw the blinking of the dull eyes and the flop of shaggy ears. He felt the coarse bristles on the broadening shoulders. Scratched them.

"I can kill you," he said quietly. "If *they* let me, I will kill you because that is why we've got you. I will hit you in the head—

there—just about there with a hammer and then I will slit your throat and hang you from that willow tree and gut you so that we, mine, can have food for a while. Do you hear me, Gussie?"

This being true there was no need to name you because from that moment when you were born, that's what life has meant for you even though you do not know it. (I did not know then, either, which of the eight would be chosen for my hand. I did not know which two would be squashed by their mammy or which four I would sell—to be killed and eaten by someone.) Nor did I know which one would be stuffed in a sack in the dark of night by a thieving wretch who more than likely if I faced him would say, with a dirty grin, "Does your wife know about your woman?"

At least the bastard did not see what happened what did not happen last night because at that very moment for all I know he was in the process of stuffing the runt into a sack. Or else watching my family squatting on the hill. Suppose he was to harm Willa Marie?

It is not the same; I did not mean to harm her, although what must she think now, but it is not the same and she wanted me and I am not like him

. . . so kind . . .

Paula's words tore at him because of how he had been with Sammy; the way he felt now—unkind, ragged inside—and Monday evening a long way off. Maybe she would not want to see him. Certainly she would not if she had seen him throw that spade.

What are you doing to do?

It is like asking Gussie what she is going to do. She is going to wallow in the mud and eat slop and corn, and grunt until one cold day when I knock her in the sloping flat senseless head with a ball-peen hammer.

There was a cool breeze, but the sun was out. The air was sharp with the scent of dying leaves, and he thought: If Jack was not dead I could take the boys squirrel hunting. I could go anyway by myself, only not to hunt squirrels but runt-hunting (and maybe see her, hold her, explain and not disappoint her again) and what if I shot him or he shot me, although I wonder if I have anything to do with that.

That day Tom Scott and I went into the Texas hills and killed twelve fox-squirrels and planned—it was late, it was in late January or February and we planned the cotton crop that was to be our best and maybe my last because I thought that I would be making cabinets and tables after I had finished my carpenter's shop and have my own business with all that rich bottom land, which Tom said would grow cotton as high as a drunk jack-rabbit's tail.

A wind blew and Tom Scott and that long-ago day when they were able to plan and choose or thought they were, was gone along with that special Texas hill and the rich bottom land and something else that George did not even bother to think about or try to remember as the ragged unpainted leaking barn loomed in front of him.

As he walked around the corner, a Colored girl looking like she was nine and a half months pregnant was in front of him saying: "Mistah, I wonders did you see a Colored gentleman around these ways?"

"No."

"He cut. He mought've been bleeding."

"Did you walk all the way from the Quarters?"

"Yassuh. I looking for Willie."

"Are you sick? You look like . . ."

"Yassuh. I looking for Willie. He cut . . ." She started crying.

"What happened to Willie? Who cut him?"

But she was not listening. And he saw her slumping, or he thought she was because she bent and clutched her stomach but did not go all the way to the ground; she stayed stooped, swaying, and George touched her shoulders.

Her head twisted toward him, but her eyes were rolling skyward and her great mouth sprang open and she cried out.

George caught her before she did fall and eased her down.

"Thelma! Nate!" Her face was wet, shiny as a purple egg-plant in the rain, and her lips were quivering.

"Willie," she said, "Willie, Willie. Oh, Willie."

"Lie still, now, wait. Just lie still." George shucked off his sweater and bundled it under her head. He called again. He ran into the barn, found a couple of feed-sacks, which he was spreading over her when he heard Willa Marie saying: "Go tell Mama" and saw her, coming, look back, yelling to Sammy to "Go tell Mama."

"What is it, Daddy? What's wrong?"

"Get your mama quick. This girl's having a baby. Run! Get some quilts!"

The girl was trying to get up. "I'se awright now, Mistuh. I got to find Willie."

"That'll have to wait," George said. He wiped her brow with his handkerchief. "Just lie still."

"Nawsuh, I . . ."

"Can you walk? Here, see if you can stand." Gently, his hands under her arms, George lifted her. "Help me," he said to Thelma who was wiping flour off her hands. "Where's Nate?"

"He's coming. What on earth . . ."

"Her baby's coming. We got to get her to the house."

"We can't . . ."

"We got to. Willa Marie, go fix a pallet in the front room. Tell Nate to draw some water."

Before they got to the house, the pains seized her again, and the four of them—George, Thelma, Nate, and Willa Marie—carried her the rest of the way and laid her on a pallet.

"It's like with a calf," whispered George to Nathan. "You remember when Bessie had trouble and you helped? Take my knife here and sharpen it. Then scald it. Get things ready, Thelma. Sammy, look after Mary Sue and Ralphie. You little ones go back yonder."

George knelt beside the girl, who was quiet again, and laid

his hand lightly on her stomach. "You just have to trust me," he said quietly. "We're going to help you. My wife and daughter will be here. You tell us. Just lie still, and I'll go wash my hands."

"Willie . . ."

"We'll find Willie when this is all over. Willa Marie? Bring me that rubbing alcohol out of the kitchen cabinet. Thelma, you look after her while I get myself clean." He started away, turned and knelt again. "You'll have to help us," he said. "Tell us and try not to be afraid. What's your name?"

"Rosa."

"That's pretty," George said. He was rolling his sleeves.

"Willa Marie, get Rosa a pillow off our bed. Bring two."

#

# Chapter 10

His own feelings during all of this (even with her crying, scream-
ing, wailing so that the very room seemed tornado-struck, or like
a coal-train had crashed through) was what he would remember:
the sure way he was, how certain he felt about what to do for Rosa,
although she was little and it was as though the baby were clogged,
unmoving.

Screams echoed, bounced off the walls, and she clawed
him, but he spoke gently to her through it all. Although Thelma
whispered, "She's going to die!" and Willa Marie cried and then
vomited, he was there when the head like a blob of bloody dough,
was suddenly there, too, as he had known with certainty it would
be, although he did not know or even think about it until Willa
Marie, when the wet, shut-eyed face emerged, said: "It's white."

George, even then, with joy filling him because it was happening and happening at his hand, taking a few seconds to see
that, yes, it was, not white, but red anyway, least of all black, but he
did not assimilate this either. He let the head rest in his palms and,
speaking gently to Rosa, received the new life as though it were
a diamond and, with a reverence never before known in any act,
deposited it at last on Rosa's stomach.

So that in the dark when Thelma asked, "What are you
going to do?" it was still not urgently important, or at least did not
erase the way he felt any more than did the knowledge that she,

Rosa, and the Colored baby who was not Colored, were at this moment lying on the pallet in his front room.

"She can't stay here."

"Did you want me to put her out in the barn?"

"Well, she sure can't stay here. Even if it was black."

This last having been discussed from a different perspective, Thelma, as she hunkered in that alcove where she milked, saying: "You sure you hadn't seen her before?"

"Not 'til I walked around the corner of the barn."

"Well, it's mighty peculiar—her coming here of all places—and it white."

"I didn't have no choice. I didn't have opportunity even if I'd thought about it to ask 'What color's it going to be?' And I had nothing to do with it being any color, and you know it."

"It's the kids I'm thinking about. And . . . them."

"Who's them?"

"Folks! What they'll say. You know how they are."

"I did what had to be done." He held out his hands, looked at his spread fingers. "I reckon I did a pretty good job. Reckon I was a fair doctor."

"It's a pity you didn't make a doctor!"

George looked down the hill, across the pasture, toward the slope where he had buried Jack (this bringing the shadow in a way that the baby's being white and that Rosa's saying: let me stay with you, White Folks, I can wash and scrub, had not) and he thought of how the alcohol had smelled, how it had felt to squeeze the cloths, slice the cord and knot it; how he had felt as he did all the right things. A quiet pride filled him while the sun disappeared and shadows swept in from the railroad.

Now: that night: "We can't afford it if nothing else."

"I'll take her home. I couldn't kick her out."

"She says her mammy won't let her come home. Says her mammy is who cut Willie."

"Appears she cut the wrong Willie."

"You ought to have got a doctor."

"I reckon. I just did what I knew needed doing."

"They're bound to come looking. If it was a girl of mine I'd be out looking for her."

"You haven't cut your girl's boyfriend with a razor, either."

"That's something, too. Where is he? What happened to him? If you ask me, you're begging for trouble."

"I don't have to beg. I can just stand still for two minutes and it'll find me."

It wasn't just that, either, George thought, meaning the way he had felt in the role of doctor. It was seeing the baby, although why it ought to have meant anything under the circumstances, why I should welcome anything new into this hard world, I don't know. But I felt it. Like it was right, that baby coming, like it was supposed to be and has nothing to do with the way things are. Now.

"You didn't have to do that." Thelma's voice was softer.

"What?"

"How you talked to her. A lot of men wouldn't have. Especially not her. You was kind to her. The way I used to hear you talk to baby calves."

Later—after the train had passed, blowing its long whistle at the crossing, wail stretching down the tracks past where Jack lay, and Thelma was relaxed beside him but jerking when the baby in the other room whimpered—George was not sleepy. I thought, when I still thought it was Willie, about me. How, was it the same with me wanting Paula. Maybe it was, only Paula is not fifteen years old, which I'll bet a dollar Rosa is not over that, and Paula wants— wanted—me. Still. Have I violated her decency in the same way? Or put her in the same category as this fifteen-year-old girl who gave in voluntarily (or was talked into it or maybe forced by somebody who cared only about the fact that he wanted) and me with a wife and five kids!

Although I cannot honestly say God I'm sorry because I would be lying. Because right now, if I was there with her whispers like quiet wind in the pines, knowing that she was lying down for me I would still and right now want her so much and not just for myself, either. Since I'm as guilty as if I had, why could I not at least have had what would have no more violated decency than what I did. Tried to do.

It's not the same, how I feel. I know how I would feel even if I knew I would never lie down with her again, if I could only see, talk to her. If I could know she cares about me and I could care about her, do something for her. Protect her from that hog-stealing bastard, from all the grinning hog-stealing bastards. If I could know and have some part in guaranteeing that she would be all right for the rest of her life, even if that meant her being happy with her sailor, though I want her this minute and will always when I think about how she—about that minute when she turned and I was sure I would kiss her. When I think of her on tip-toe, her mouth . . .

I felt so good and smooth and right birthing that baby (he was "talking" to Paula about it now); I have always liked how it smells in doctors' offices, and I had an easy way about me when I used to doctor sick animals and today, yesterday (whenever I get to talk to her about today) when I held, saw, that head emerging and heard the screams, in spite of that, it was like sitting somewhere safe while a cyclone was howling some place else. I . . .

He heard the baby cry. Rosa moved in the other room. He heard the house creak, smelled the close tight staleness and couldn't stop thinking of the stolen pig and Jack. I cannot ever be a doctor. What happened today just did. I cannot even have a cabinet-shop or own ten good acres or even get my runt of a pig back, though I have to try, and what exactly do I plan to do about that girl in there who wants to stay with us?

I works good, she said. Thelma is right about **them,** too; even though ordinarily not a one of the neighbors would step across the road to do anything except borrow, now they will. He may at this minute be ripping the screen off her window or maybe crowding her into that little drafty room. (He cut Jack's throat . . .)

Later, he heard Rosa calling (voice blending unobtrusively with darkness but flowing to his ear), unmistakably saying: Willie . . . Her baby cried—one tiny sharp cry in the night, before, he guessed, she stuck a smoky nipple in his mouth—and that cry touched George in a very lonely way and was tied in, somehow, with what he felt when he first saw the head ballooning out of her body. Only now, he was lonely. Knowing: We all came out of darkness on schedule. For what? To cry, for hunger, for pain? We feel. We do feel. That is the one sure thing.

Out of the deep tired sleep which finally took him, George heard a knocking as though someone was hammering, and his dream-apparatus flickered a Texas scene: Tom Scott nailing rafters; this shattered by Thelma's gripping hand and whisper: "Somebody's at the door!"

Shadow against shadow, body gradually materializing close so that he thought maybe he should have heeded Thelma's advice about getting his gun, but it was too late. He could make out now the broad shoulders, and he heard, "Is you got Rosa?"

"Who are you?"

"Willie. Is you got Rosa?"

#

# Chapter 11

George heard singing from the church a half mile away as he unlatched the rusty gate and stepped into the wet, shaded place leading to the house. Speckled chickens scurried around the untrimmed hedge. A caisson lay close to the porch, its circle filled with dirt and the dead stems of last summer's flowers. A slatted swing, once green, hung on the narrow porch. A skinny black and brown puppy with tail tucked between its legs whimpered under the window. This was where Willie—after he had eaten and talked with Rosa, and George had treated the puckered gash on his cheek—had told him he would find Rosa's mama.

George heard the voices floating on the air and a piano from the church I am bound for the pra-ham-ised land—Hallelujah . . . as he stepped on to the porch. Dark wet soil smell mixed with the aroma of collards cooking.

"Come on."

He heard the voice after he had knocked, but he did not open the door. A stained curtain hung limp against the inside glass. He knocked again.

"Come on."

A car with a bad exhaust bumped across the bridge. George gripped the loose doorknob, turned until it caught, and pushed.

"What is it?"

First, he saw the iron bedstead, then two children on the bed.

"What you want?"

He followed the voice and saw the woman lying on a low ragged sofa with a towel across her head. She moved the towel higher so she could see. Her elbow pointed toward him like a shotgun.

"It's about Rosa . . ." George began. "This where she lives?"

The small heater near the woman's head gave off strong heat, flames shooting behind the slits. There was a close stuffiness in the room.

"Rosa?"

"Yes, Ma'am. Are you her mama?"

"What you want, Mistah?"

"Rosa had her baby. At my house."

"Lawdy mercy!" Her arms went up again to lay across her face. She groaned. The kids whispered. A boy, about eight, had appeared in the inner doorway. The arm moved, came down, and her head turned.

"What you called?"

"George Malone."

"Where you stay?"

"Down the road, half mile. Next to the railroad."

"Lawdy." She moved. Sat. "Mistah Malone, I been worried sick about that chile. You say she done had that baby?"

"Yes ma'am. They're all right. It's a boy." Little white boy, but you know that. You know a lot more than I know and you know too that I know about Willie. He told her why Rosa was at his house with her baby.

"Willie at yo' place?"

"Not now. We fed him breakfast about four o'clock and he left. He told me how to find you."

"I reckon he know."

"I don't have a car to bring Rosa home, but I wanted you to know she is all right."

"I appreciates that, Mistah Malone. And what y'all done for my little girl. I been worried sick all night. I ain't got no man. Just these little chilren. And Rosa."

"I thought maybe you could get somebody to bring her home."

"Yassuh, I reckon that's what we do, only I don't know who."

She spoke to the children and they scampered off the bed, into the back. The older boy stood in the doorway, until she said: "Raymond, you get away." She got to her feet and pulled a curtain to seal off the back. "Mistah Malone, I got to ask you something. About Rosa's baby."

"Yes'm," George said. "He's white."

Her head moved from side to side. "Mmmmmm-hmmm-mm, Lawdy, Lawdy!" She came to George, standing straight with her hands on her huge hips, upper arms sagging like sand in wet sacks. "Did Willie tell how come he be bleeding?"

"He said you cut him."

"I had to, Mistah Malone, on account of what he fixing to do. Onliest way I could keep Willie from being sent off. Or 'lectro-cuted. Onliest way I could keep Willie from going over there toting a pia-stol. Lawdy mercy, I don't know . . ."

"Over where?" asked George, hoping she wouldn't point in the direction where she did point.

"He fo'ced her. He fo'ced my Rosa."

(Although it did not necessarily mean just because she pointed in the general direction of the road where Paula lived and where, apparently, the dark grinning runt-stealing low-life bastard also lived, that she was referring to him.) Only she was because after George asked "Who?" and she said: "Tatum" and he still did not know, he kept questioning until there was no doubt.

He wanted to get it settled quickly about how to get Rosa and her baby home and get back to things that concerned him, pri-marily at that moment running down the road to see with certainty that she was all right and that she too had not (sometime since that long-ago rainy night when he had failed her) been forced by the man whose name he now knew.

He thought of something, and he grabbed it as if it would make any difference because, even if the black woman in whose house he now stood (never having been invited to sit although he had a few hours earlier delivered her daughter's bastard son), even if she was wrong it would not mean that Paula was any safer from being forced, but still he said: "I thought he just moved back there a short while ago."

"Did. Right after we moved heah. Befoah, lived in Black-water, too, and he fo'ced Rosa, then followed her here."

"Willie said if she could come home he'd find somebody to bring them, but he didn't know if you'd let him."

"You tell Willie to bring my baby home."

"It may be a day or two."

"Yassuh, I understands that. You tell Willie to bring both my babies home."

George turned, wanting to run. Wanting to free himself from the closeness, the suffocating room, and from the fear that could only be cured by knowing that Paula was safe.

"I thanks you for what you done . . ."

"You're welcome," said George, and the fresh air hit him like a palmed hand as he left the house. He would not remember getting to the gate, going through it and on to the road where he heard a loud, melodious male voice floating, rising, falling—the Colored preacher's voice from half a mile away on that quiet Sunday morn.

\* \* \*

The house, perched on low bricks, looked lonesome, vulnerable. It's bricked in; at least he cannot crawl under it. A piece of tin covered a back kitchen window. He could not see the room where they had been, where no moonlight had shone anyway because it was raining, but he had been inside that room, and maybe soon would see it again. He walked rapidly, with the feeling that he was being watched from the Colored houses. He felt his chest tightening.

There was no smoke coming from the chimney. She did not answer his knock. He opened the screen and pressed his face against the door. The house was like an unanswered telephone.

George saw three white boys in the road, throwing rocks. George looked toward where he believed Tatum lived, wondered if those were his boys ogling him, cussing, scooping up stones and hurling them.

What do I do now? I cannot even know if she is in there. If she needs me . . .

He headed down the road, his insides tight as a fist. He knew when he saw the pig-pen at the rear of the shotgun house—a piece of tin stuck over one corner—that it was the place. A torn and yellowed mattress lay against the house. There was a chopblock with an ax caught in it, and a scattered pile of wood. Junk of all sorts cluttered the yard, and a wisp of smoke escaped toward the back.

Did she mean Willie had the pistol? Or Tatum?

He rushed through the yard, skirting the house, straight to the pen where, even before he could see over the poles, he spotted the runt—saw his snout through the poles, and verified, then, by touching the top pole and looking, yes, it was his pig. A skinny black bowed-back dried-titted sow shared the pen, front hooves in an empty trough. George grabbed the top pole, yanked, seeing the rusty wire that held it in place.

Whether he would have actually jerked the poles loose, so that the sow and runt could both be free—no thought of returning the pig to his house but wanting to destroy the pen and give the brutes a chance—George never knew. Because he heard, a few steps behind him, like fingernails sliding on slate, a voice: "What the hell you doing?" and turned, taking his time, to see the dirty whiskered face under the black cap.

"I've come for my pig."

"*Your* pig?"

George could barely see his eyes, but the crooked grin was in view. "Yes, my pig. The one you stole Friday night."

A big hand went to the nose, head turned, blowing. The face was redder than George had thought and flabbier, and he had been careless with his tobacco. There was yellow at the corners of his mouth, too. "I seen you out here at my pen and thought maybe you'd mistaken where you thought you was." Tatum walked to the opposite side, leaned on the pen, hands folded over the top pole. "Never seen you down this far before."

"That's my shoat."

If I knew you had touched her I would take that trace chain lying there and beat your filthy face to a pulp.

"So you like my little shoat? Well, he ain't for sale."

"Tatum, you stole that pig."

"How come you ain't lawed me, then?"

Which is what I would have done once, but here I've never so much as seen a deputy. Would have to ask a dozen people to find how to go about getting in touch with whoever is supposed to represent the county sheriff, in the event that somebody from Ox Hill should take the trouble to report something. "You just bring me the sack you brought him here in and step aside."

"You just hit the trail. Less'n of course you might want to stop off between here and wherever it is you live." Tatum moved his arms from the pole and looked toward the patch of oaks below his house. George heard him spitting.

I could say: Maybe the law would like to know, too, what you did to that girl, only the law wouldn't be interested except maybe to laugh and drive out of their way to get a peek and maybe get some notion about taking their own turn with who you, Tatum, consider to be just a "little niggah gal."

"Does your old lady know about your little woman?" Tatum said it without looking at him.

George glanced again at his runt and then walked past the house. He felt swayed, tilted, wanted to turn around. Keep walking. It is exactly what you knew he would say. If you turn around you will kill him or be killed. Because there is nothing you can say. Unless you take that trace chain (and where would you stop?) keep walking because you could not say that little woman is a lady because even if you were not guilty he wouldn't understand the term (and for all you know somebody inside has a shotgun leveled at your back, only that is not the reason; at least you know it is not that you are afraid, though Tatum does not know this) but keep walking. You cannot afford to go to jail for killing a nothing like him.

Sunlight glistened in the bedroom window of her house, and George felt a lonely stab; saw the house huge as if it was the only thing on the horizon, and thought: She cannot be inside. She has to be gone. Alive and well. But what can I do if she is not?

He passed, knowing it would be at least six hours or maybe more before he could know because that was how long it would be before dark when, even then, unless there was a light in her window he would not be able to do anything except go home again.

\#

# Chapter 12

Maybe it was a blessing that they came, but only later would he think of this. Even after he saw them standing or hunkered at the edge of his yard he did not stop hurting. He did not immediately think why they were there any more than he had thought during the walk home about the Colored girl who was still in his house. Although he did think of this (and for a moment stopped thinking of Paula) when one of the men, hands inside overalls bib, stepped away from the cluster as George left the road to enter his yard, and said, "We need to talk to you."

"Reckon I don't know you," George said, although he had recognized the shorter one who was cleaning his nails with a knife-blade, or knew that he lived a mile down the road and had been there one afternoon, holding a handle of a washtub filled with coal stolen from a parked railroad car. And he knew which one was Otis Carpenter (who had sold him the red sow); also, he had seen two others, but as far as he knew, he had never seen the one who stepped out to address him.

"Name's Higgins. I'm your neighbor. We all your neighbors."

"Well, then, would you like to come inside?"

"I reckon not, seeing as how some of us are kinda ticky about being in houses with niggahs."

"Suit yourself," George said. "I reckon it ain't too chilly to set on the porch."

"What we got to say can be said right chere. What you aiming to do about your niggah gurl?"

"You talking about the young woman?"

"Wye yea." He blinked, turned and looked sharply at the others, blinked at George. "Yeah, that's who I meant. How many niggahs you got in there?"

"Didn't say I had any."

"Didn't need to," said Carpenter.

"You can't hide a niggah," the shorter one said.

"I'm not trying to hide anybody or anything," said George, vexed at having to explain what should not have to be explained. Only this was not a band of tramps passing through; these were neighbors. And so, as he had forced himself to walk away from Tatum, he forced himself to stand silently, absorbing glares and sidelong glances.

"We just wanted to tell you, neighborly like, that you ought to be careful about who you let in your house," Higgins said. He fished a pipe from somewhere, stuffed tobacco and lit it.

"She had a baby."

"We know that."

"Seems you know a lot about something that's in my house considering that, far as I know, none of you ever set foot in it."

"We know you got a niggah gal in there that's dropped a kid, which if we hear correct ain't exactly what you'd call coal black."

"I didn't choose for her to pick my yard to have her baby."

"Maybe that ain't no accident," the shorter one said, snickering. "Considering how the kid as I understand looks like it coulda been dunked in a barrel of flair."

Gordon's not here, thought George, although later when Thelma told him that one of the Gordon kids had come to borrow something, he knew how the word had spread. "Men, I did what I had to do," he said. "I'd never seen the girl 'til she came to my barn, looking . . ." He stopped. "Pains hit her, and we did what needed to be done. I'm sorry if that bothers you." He started to step around Higgins.

"We ain't got nothing agin you, understand," said Higgins. "We just thought, being neighbors and all, we ought to tell you. Some of us been around these parts longer than you, and we figure you just not on to our ways here in Ox Hill."

"Maybe one of you would like to provide transportation to take her home," George said. He looked at the green Chevrolet parked beside the road. "I got no car myself."

"Hell," the short one said. "Let her get home the way she got here."

"I reckon I'll do whatever I think needs doing," George said.

He was almost to the porch when Higgins called, "Don't make no mistake, now. You don't want to make no mistake. We'uns your neighbors, even though we ain't black."

Keep walking. Keep walking now. And he entered his house (it was like walking into shade on a blistering August day) and saw, in a rocking chair nursing her baby, the Colored girl while Willa Marie sat cross-legged on the floor, watching.

"Your mama says Willie can bring you home," George said.

"I wants to stay here. I works good."

#

·

# Chapter 13

As George walked home that night he almost wished he had not gone back to Paula's house. But at least now he knew that she was all right; that she had gone to Willis in the afternoon to see a picture show. So that part was all right, that fear erased.

Now there was a new worry. There always was something new, something not right, unfinished, so that he never could feel complete about it.

There was never time—there had not been time enough to properly tell about Tatum and Rosa and Rosa's white son and how he had felt (how wonderful) delivering the baby—no time to explain how he had walked away that morning without doing anything to protest Tatum's remark about her, no time to tell about the delegation in his yard. He had failed her again, too. This was the new guilt and shame and frustration, which canceled whatever good his going back had accomplished.

A line of light had glowed beneath the bottom of the door in that back room, but he had moved too quickly and, as he approached the velvet moment (trying not to think of that other time, finding confidence in the very readiness that would be his downfall) the sudden shower came, unstoppable, over. Empty silence, then whispers.

"It doesn't matter." She kissed his cheek. She moved his

arm so she could lie inside it.

"I've wanted you so much."

"You have me."

* * *

Thelma was rocking the baby and humming when he got home. Rosa lay on her pallet, facing Thelma and the baby. Her face was streaked with tears.

"What's wrong?"

Thelma shook her head. "Shh. He's nearly asleep."

"You sick, Rosa?"

She was drawn up on the quilts like a wounded animal, sobbing.

"She's worried about Willie. He's in jail."

"Jail?"

"A Colored boy rode up on a mule from Blackwater, said Willie broke into the Commissary last night. Shhh, now, shhh, go to sleep, Arthur Dee."

Arthur Dee. This caught his attention (rather than the fact that Willie, who was to take Rosa home, was in jail)—the discovery that the baby had been named. That this scared black girl had named her baby. Yes. Even though he is only here because that thieving low-life crawled her, he has a name. Must have a name. For he is now one of us.

"The boy thought they took him to the Willis jail."

George knelt beside Rosa. "Where does Willie live?" Remembering, he asked: "Where does he **stay**?"

"With Peggy Lee."

"In Blackwater?"

"Yassuh."

"Who's Peggy Lee?"

"His sistah." Tears flowed. George glanced at Thelma,

looked at the flickering lamp.

What does this have to do with me? Through what choosing, on my part, is this girl lying on my floor and her baby dozing in my wife's arms and her Willie in jail and Tatum popping up every which way I turn, this bumping into Tatum who even now may be crawling through her window . . .

Brown darkened knot-holed boards of the room looked unfamiliar; that he should be here of all places; that this should be his house, and even so not his.

"Don't cry. We'll take care of you 'til you feel better."

She did not look at him but scooted back a little and her hand moved, smoothing flour-sack sheet, making a place for Thelma to lay the sleeping Arthur Dee. She covered him with a faded baby blanket, which George remembered buying in McKenzie's Mercantile in Horton, Texas, the day Sammy was born. The same blanket.

"Are you warm enough, Rosa?"

"Yassuh."

Just a flicker, then, as he stood about to turn away. He saw her face, caught, focused on her for the first time not as Colored Girl. He studied the broad forehead beyond the prune skin and saw the structure—the rounded cheekbones, high brow hooding deep-set eyes—the plaited wire-like coils of black hair. All of this he had seen but not seen. Until now. Now, in that flicker, recognizing her as a woman, bitten already by the invisible bug that would bite harder every day of her life.

In that stopped second, George knew that Rosa would be lucky if she could always answer yes to the question: Are you warm? He saw (in that frozen fraction of time when he did not see black skin) a woman, one who could feel pain.

Those goofy neighbors of mine! I could have a sick dinosaur, a monster, in my house, he thought, and they wouldn't care. But not Rosa.

*** * ***

"What are you going to do?" asked Thelma in the darkness, when the house was without light except (although he could not see it) a glow from a dying fire in the room where Rosa and her baby lay. In the dark, George thought of Jonah in the fish's belly.

In this house I lay me down

And Rosa is part of it. Inside. Asking to stay inside with us, asking only for the privilege to work and let that baby (Tatum's baby) suck; that baby that happened to her not with pleasure but as the leftover of pain, already one of us. Named.

"He's a pretty baby," Thelma said.

"She was raped. Her mammy told me."

"Who did it?"

"Some low-down white man." I cannot tell Thelma who. Tatum, although he wouldn't need an excuse, knows or thinks he knows all he needs to know to justify whatever he might choose to do. As he must have justified raping Rosa on the grounds that she is a "nigger" although he would not think it necessary to justify his action other than that he wanted, wants.

"Y'all use the slop-jar after dark. Don't go outside at night."

"That girl's using it."

Yes. I forgot that she's Colored, and this slop-jar business would bother you. "I'll buy another one tomorrow."

George lay awake, turning over certain moments like sorting marbles. His life had become isolated moments, which he took out one at a time to look at. Paula. And that bright moment when he had sliced the baby's bloody cord. And that other moment also came back, the minute when the quick thundershower robbed them again.

He recalled the feeling that came over him in his flickering recognition of Rosa as a human being, and how he had glimpsed what her life would be—how it was that she, if she could, would choose his miserable lot over hers.

It was black in the house. Not a thin bright line of light anywhere.

# Chapter 14

"What is it?" asked Thelma, before dawn, when George raised off his pillow.

"Somebody's up. I heard somebody in the kitchen." Although it may have been his nose, rather than his ears, that had awakened him because Thelma, also sitting now, said, "I smell meat frying."

She saw first—it was her kitchen, and curiosity (about who had invaded that personal last-private thing, which indisputably belonged to her) overpowered any fear that by rushing through that door she might jeopardize her safety. She came back as George dressed, and whispered: "She's cooking our breakfast!"

Rosa, in the loose flannel gown that Thelma had loaned or maybe given to her, reminded him of Willa Marie—the way she used to dress up in Thelma's clothes. Rosa, with the baby clutched against her shoulder, was tending a skillet at the wood stove.

"What are you doing?" asked Thelma, although strips of fatback fried and laid on a china platter, and broken egg-shells on the flat stove-top answered that.

"Cooking for y'all." She turned, using part of the baggy sleeve as a potholder, lifted the pot and poured coffee into two mugs.

"Did you build the fire, too?" Thelma had moved closer, not looking at Rosa, but at what she had done; seeing two plates and mugs on the table; counting four egg-shells. Oven door closed on baking biscuits.

"Yes'm. Y'all want gravy?"

"I'll make it, Rosa."

"Here's eggs." Scraping three fourths of the yellow glob on to George's plate.

"Why, I . . ." Thelma looked at George. She brushed her hair back and went to the cabinet for the sugar bowl. "Well."

George went outside to relieve his bladder. Light was breaking. The sulfuric scent from Blackwater lay heavy on the air. He was cold in his shirt sleeves, but he was glad to see a clear sky with no hint of rain.

Morning. Safe new morning with many things obscured for a while; short reprieve from yesterday. Not just breakfast, George thought, coming back in, but "for y'all."

Rosa stood near the stove while they ate.

"Do you go to school, Rosa?" Knowing she could not have gone.

"Nawsuh. My brothers do. And sister."

"How many brothers and sisters?"

"Foah."

They would not care about Rosa being here if she worked for us. They do not know what they care about. They have never seen her as I saw her last night. Thelma hasn't, either. Yet. Though she has heard her cry.

He split a golden biscuit—its insides puffy like a boll of cotton. He buttered it and reached for the syrup.

It is the cry that does it.

It is the cry that tells that they—we—can feel. It is the cry that says who we are. It's the cry inside when I think of *her*, maybe waking up right now by herself. (It is the tiny cry she makes when we kiss.)

"Fix yourself some breakfast, Rosa. I'll take care of the children when they get up. Here, give me the baby."

Rosa did not give up the baby, but she did pour gravy on a biscuit, take a piece of meat and a mug of coffee and go out of the room. She won't eat with us. I don't know how she sees us.

"She's worried they'll shoot Willie. She wants you to see about him."

"Me?"

"While you were out, she said 'Can he hep Willie?'"

"I can't help nobody," he almost shouted.

He ate very fast, drained the mug, held it as Thelma refilled it. "I can't lose the time. What does she expect me to do, anyway? I can't bail him out. I don't even know where the jail is. It's not like Willie was a white man! They don't care . . ."

"She's scared they have shot him."

"Aw . . ."

"I'm just telling you. She's your project. I reckon she thinks you can fix anything."

"I got to go." He gulped coffee. "I can't fix nothing!"

Only if I could go to Willis I could see Paula and see where she works, and we could walk together. Or if I went tonight, I could see her after.

As he went through the front room—Rosa on the pallet, not facing him, sopping gravy—George paused at the door. "Willie will be all right," he said.

"They going shoot Willie," she said.

"They won't shoot him, Rosa."

"Can you hep Willie, Mistah Malone?"

Maybe Thursday. Thanksgiving. Maybe I can go then just so I can tell Rosa he is still alive.

"I . . ." He went to the kitchen door. "If I . . . in case I should be late tonight, I might go check on him."

"Big surprise," his wife answered.

#

# Chapter 15

George stepped off the bus on the rounded curb next to the First National Bank of Birmingham in Willis. A railroad split the street in front of the bank. The bus had crossed it, and George saw the big X's of the crossing, lights not red now. Ought to be bright now warning because there is no telling what I'm getting into, assuming I can find the jail. I did not come here primarily to see Willie, though see is the most I could hope for, and I do want to help Rosa but would I be here if it had not been the chance it gives me to maybe see Paula later?

He saw the double row of light-bulbs in front of the picture show across the tracks and wondered how it would be to go to a movie with Paula. This old town makes me think of her because she works here, has walked, stood, right where I'm standing. Catches the bus here, I know.

George approached an old man in a police uniform, not knowing whether he was a Willis officer or a bank watchman. "Excuse me, Uncle, I wonder if you could tell me where the jail is."

"I'm not your uncle!" The eyes under the shaggy brows glowered.

"I didn't mean any offense. Where I used to live, 'Uncle' was a sign of respect to an old . . ."

"I ain't old!" he snapped. He began to move on, as though George were the fireplug or iron-green mailbox beside the bank.

George started away, too.

"Jail's over yonder. Backa that dadburn building."

George walked down the narrow street: A Hills grocery store was on his right, though closed, everything closed, including the Five & Dime Store where she worked. He tried to visualize her standing behind one of the counters, and he felt lonesome as he looked down the empty aisles (lonesome for her, too, being in that unfriendly town); yet somehow feeling better as he walked to the corner and cut through an alley, trying to think of what he would say if he did find the miserable Willie.

Worn stone steps led into the dingy jail office. Windows on both floors were barred. The door leading to the office had a stained-glass panel halfway up, so that he saw light. Behind a desk sat a fat man, WPD in silver stuck on the blue wool, freckled hand holding a telephone receiver. A woman in a coat with a rabbit collar—an old coat that partially covered a print dress above coarse cotton stockings and once-black oxfords—sat at one end of the office on a short pew. At the other end, on a green boarded wall, were posters of fugitives.

"Did you want something?" The brown eyes were aloof, like the eyes behind unemployment desks. Like the Blackwater doctor's.

"Yes sir. I was wondering if I could see a man you have here—Colored man." Suddenly remembering, realizing, that he did not know Willie's last name. ". . . who I understand was supposed to have broken into the Commissary over at Blackwater. Willie."

"When was this supposed to have happened?"

"It would have been, I guess, Saturday night."

"Did he work for you?"

"No sir. I just . . ."

The eyes were checking him out, showing a slight interest.

"Where do you live, Mister? You live in Blackwater?"

"No sir, I live up the hill from Blackwater."

"Ox Hill?"

George nodded.

How to answer? How to say: He is nothing to me but he is something to a young girl (also Colored) who happened to pick my yard to have her white baby in, which was necessary, not because of the man you have locked up back there, but because of a mangy no-good white man who probably will never be arrested, or at least certainly not for crawling a Colored girl, and even if I told you he stole my shoat, probably not even then. Not for long, anyway.

"I was just wondering if I could see him for a minute and maybe talk with him. You see . . ."

"You talking about that niggah who busted outta the back door of the jail this afternoon? That who you mean? Willie Jerdan? That who you wanting to see?"

\#

# Chapter 16

He saw lights when he got off the bus, but of course he could not see her house. He thought: Thank goodness she has lights and water, which is more than I've got. Three-quarters of a mile either way, and I would have lights and water if I could afford them, but I'm in between.

By living between the Quarters and the heart of Ox Hill community, he forfeited the choice, since whether he could pay was not relevant to the greater issue of whether enough other people living in that in-between stretch could justify extending either service, and they—some aloof, tie-wearing They—had determined that too few people lived there to justify the expense.

George did not think long about the lights (and he could not think totally about Paula, even though eagerness was winding tighter with every step), but he could not shut out the thought of the Willis jail or knowing that Willie—whom he had only seen once and now knew was Willie Jerdan—that this hulking Willie who had eaten four o'clock breakfast in his kitchen, had escaped.

Of more immediate concern were the questions he had been asked by the officer and a man in a suit (with a pistol on his hip) who said he was chief deputy of the county. For a while he had thought they would lock him up as replacement for "that big buck niggah of your'n" whose escape was somehow supposed to have been George's fault.

He tried, as he turned off the main road, to concentrate on Paula—the prime, although almost lost reason for his being subjected to the questioning, though she did not know this—but there was something lodged, like a bone in the throat, in his brain: Maybe I ought not to have told them about Rosa at all. Or maybe I ought to have told them everything. Having said only, "She works for us," which was not a lie since she had that morning cooked their breakfast, although it was not because of wanting to lie or thwart their search, or to interfere in any way with their pursuit of justice, but only because he had not seen clearly a way to tell them: I delivered her baby.

He glanced in the direction of the house where he had visited on Sunday morning and wondered what effect his telling would have on Rosa's mama, or on what she thought of him since there was, unrecognized almost, a feeling that she held a good image of him because he had helped her daughter. He wondered what he might have done to that image. But he was, at last, going to see Paula and to hold her and talk—to fill in all the gaps, to tell (this was part of their relationship, how there always was something unfinished, something to tell; some urgent need to share something they both carried through the day or days, held on to, saved to share, in whatever brief time they might have together). He felt the glow as he approached the bridge, first moving to the roadside to let a car pass. Only it did not pass.

George saw his shadow spring crookedly from the left of the bridge forward and to the other side, caught in the glare of headlights, which meant that whoever was behind him was not concerned about which side of the road to drive on, but was in fact easing up behind George, swerving, then, as he turned—in that moment seeing the unlit bubble in the center of the top of the black car—bubble unlighted, like the railroad crossing signs had been, but even so, warning.

The car pulled alongside George, and the man with the pistol on his hip rolled the window down and said: "Howdy."

"Yes sir?"

Light from in front of the store cut across the face, exposing sharp nose and smile, although George also could see in shadows, the eyes that, in the station, had glinted (like sun hitting an ax blade on a cold day), and with him in the car, another deputy.

"Where you going?"

"Home."

"You live back here, do you?"

"No sir, I live down the road apiece."

"How's come you going this way then?"

"I was going to cut down the tracks. It's closer."

"You mean you come up here to walk down the tracks to get home, steada keeping to the road?"

"Sometimes."

The teeth picked up light. The smile was still in place. Only the eyes, in shadows, moved. "You seen our niggah?"

"No sir, sure haven't. I just got off the bus."

"Know you did. You sure you not heading over here to see him?"

"I told you, Sheriff, I'm trying to get home."

The other man said something.

"Yeah," the chief deputy said, chuckling. "Leo wants to know if maybe you planning on hopping a train, reason you taking the tracks." He laughed. "Come on, get in, Malone. I'll take you home."

The car rumbled across the bridge, turned—as though to go to her house. George, in the back seat, anxiously looked down the twin barrels of light seeing, as the car backed, a streak of light in her window.

Almost. Three or four minutes more, and I would have been in her house. But it's a good thing I wasn't since they were parked somewhere watching. Which means . . .

"How long this black gal been working for you? Willie's gal."

Suddenly the back seat was crowded. Tatum. Down the road, Tatum, is who they wanted, who they ought to have driven a quarter of a mile on down the road to drag out of bed and stick in the back seat. Tatum who stole a pig and raped a young girl. Lord knows what else. Me? Me? In here with these men?

"Say?"

"Not long."

"How long?"

George sighed. "She come down last Saturday."

"Mm-hmmm. Where she live?"

"Quarters, I reckon."

Quiet. Lord, the power of quiet. Waiting to see if they took it. Accepted it. Neither officer said anything, until the car slowed, as it approached his house. George noticed although they had not asked where he lived.

"This your place coming up?"

"Yes."

With lights still on, focusing on the trunk of a big oak in the corner of George's yard, the chief deputy turned, laying his arm on the back of the seat in front of George. "I hear she lives with you."

"She's just . . . staying here!" George said. (Remembering Rosa's mama saying: "Where you stay?" he thought: Maybe that's why.)

The driver laughed. He turned so that he could see George, or so George could see him, could know without a light that the teeth showed and the eyes glinted.

"That your little baby sucking her black tit?"

"No!"

"What I hear, he's white enough he could be. That right?"

"Look, officers. Let me tell you what happened. I was coming up from the pasture Saturday. Me and the boys had buried our dog. Some—somebody cut his throat Friday night. Carried off a little shoat of mine and cut my dog's throat . . ."

"You turn that in?"

"No. I got no phone."

"Could rode a bus, like you did today, hunting your niggah . . ."

"I was coming up from the pasture and when I came around the barn, she was standing there. I'd never laid eyes on her before in my life . . ."

He told all of it then. About the baby, about Willie coming and eating breakfast, about visiting Rosa's mama and planning to get Rosa home as soon as she was well.

"She cooked breakfast for us this morning." He wished he had not said that; felt somehow he had let the men enter a part of his life that they should never enter. "That's why I said she works for me. She wants to stay and work . . ."

"How come you didn't tell us this before?"

"I don't know." He was tired of it. "I didn't think it was important. I don't know anything about Willie Jerdan. I just did what I thought needed doing. And that's the truth."

"Malone, you said you work on a project. That's what you told Officer Simmons, wasn't it? What kinda work you do?"

"I'm a carpenter." This was good. This was the only good thing that had happened all night, being able to say: I'm a carpenter.

"How long you been here?"

"Since October, year ago."

"Where'd you come from before that?"

"Louisiana. I'm from Texas."

"Whereabouts?"

"Horton. But I got work down below Shreveport. Played out. I worked in Mississippi nearly a year. Moved here. Year ago October."

"Well, how come me to ask is that I don't know if you know how it is around these parts. Around here they don't—we don't hold no truck with living with niggahs."

"I . . ."

"I ain't aiming to ride you, Malone. I believe you. I just thought I'd tell you as a favor. I didn't know how long exactly you might have been here. You don't want no trouble." He lighted a cigarette, blew smoke, glanced over his shoulder. "That boy will likely come smelling around your place long as that little bitch is here. You see him, let us know, will you?"

"All right," George said. The ground felt good.

"Good night, now," the chief deputy said as the tires ground into gravel, swung and headed back in the direction of the Quarters.

#

# Chapter 17

Whether it was the shot or Rosa's screams he would never know because it seemed that both happened simultaneously, tearing his sleep with one clean swipe. He knew later that the shot must have come first. The scream did not end any more than a train's whistle ends the second the cord is released. Before it had faded through the dark house, it was followed by a low continuous wail. This wail, rising, flowing like burning oil, overshadowed the other crying, which it produced, and it was the wail rather than Arthur Dee's squalls that burnt into George's memory.

The sounds filled the house, chilled George so that even after he was in the room with her (pulling on his overalls quickly and peering through a window toward the barn, toward where the other sound had been) his scalp prickled. "Shhh." But this was futile. Thelma clutched his arm. Everybody, it seemed, was in the room.

"What happened?"

"Y'all listen." He was trying to see. He stretched his hand toward Rosa in a useless gesture. "Get a match. No, don't. Just be still. Get my gun, Nate. Shhh. See if you can get her quiet."

Thelma got the baby, bouncing him lightly on her shoulder, patting, until his crying stopped abruptly, making Rosa's sounds seem louder.

"Y'all stay put. Try to hush her, Thelma."

"Don't go out there!"

But he had opened the door. "Give me my gun." Light was flickering—yellow sky breaking—though part of this was glare from the Marbletown furnaces. George crept across the porch, stopped, aware then that Nathan was behind him. "You stay here."

"Be careful, Daddy."

George saw the car (saw black hulk inside black of night, parked on the edge of the road in front of the barn) seconds before pieces of blood-red light began to whirl across the yard, into trees, against house—the flashing red light atop the sheriff's car lighting up the front of the barn, spraying the dark shadows hovering near the barn. One shadow held a flashlight; played it.

"Go back inside, Nate. Here. Take this." For I do not need a gun. Now. Slivers of red reminded him of fire he had seen falling from coal-trains in the night, scattering into weeds.

I do not have to go out there to find out. I already know. But he stepped off the porch, took the dirt steps down a bank to the lower path leading to the barn. Rosa's cries followed him.

He did not hurry. He walked, unfeeling, not thinking that he might be a target, or that they did not already know that he was there, or might not know who he was. Bits of pulsating light speckled his face just as it speckled blue suit and smiling face and speckled, too, brown uniform of another deputy and the long silver flashlight he held, pointing its own misty ray toward that very corner where George had first seen Rosa.

He saw the circle, small white-yellow circle at the end of the misty ray; saw in that circle blue denim torso and then twisted black jaw; saw Willie Jerdan's open mouth, or one side of it, because his head was twisted toward the barn. Willie was on his back. His feet—although they were not in that bright circle—pointed toward George.

"There's your niggah." This from behind, in the red-spattered darkness. The circle moved, grew larger, encompassed hips, tweed checkered breeches, partially open at the fly; wet muddy cuffs and shoe and six inches of black leg where the breeches were tugged upward, wrinkled. And one hand open so the pink palm showed. George shivered. His teeth chattered.

"He was hiding in your crib," the voice said. "Did you know?"

George hugged himself. He didn't look away. He looks short, George thought.

"Say, Malone?"

"No."

"I don't reckon you had anything to do with him being bedded down in your crib, did you?"

George shook his head, not speaking.

"Sombitch run," the deputy said. "Only he run the wrong way. Smack-dab into the sheriff."

George was conscious of the wail and thought it must never have stopped, that he was only now hearing it again, but then he realized he was hearing it because Rosa was coming down the path.

"Who's that?"

"It's Rosa."

She stopped behind them. The wailing stopped, too, for a split second, then burst from her as she ran and fell across the still Willie.

"Get her away. Go on, Leo, get her away."

"Wait," George said. "I will." Nathan was there, too, now, and Thelma; they were there, helping him tug at Rosa.

"Y'all can't get her, we can."

Rosa still clung but allowed George to move her back into Thelma's arms.

"She's cold," George told his wife. "She doesn't have any shoes on. Y'all get her to the house."

Suddenly they didn't need the flashlight. Darkness was peeling away, falling off the sky.

"What did he take?" George asked the deputy. "When he

broke into the Commissary, what was it he took?" He was having difficulty speaking, his voice breaking in cadence with his chattering teeth.

"Loaf of bread, I reckon. That's what they said, ain't it, Sheriff? Loaf of bread?"

"My God," George said. "How much is a loaf of bread worth?"

"Well, about a dime, I reckon. Or nickel. Depending on the size."

George turned away. Something was missing, his shirt was not moving, the ground had no bright spots.

"You'll stay close, won't you Malone?" the deputy asked. He was coming from the car, having turned off the red light. "You won't be going nowhere directly on account of we'll need to ask you some questions. Go ahead, eat you some breakfast. And, hey, you better get that gal outta your house. You see what kind of trouble they can cause."

George was aware, without looking, that the other deputy was relieving himself. There at the corner of the barn.

#

# Chapter 18

By late afternoon—when George went that way, stepping around the place where Willie had lain—it was like a dream. Blown large, an unreal sadness that crowded out everyday feelings.

It was the way he had felt when his mother died. It was the way people are in those first few suspended hours after a death, when they are lifted out of themselves.

The ax he carried felt unusually large and while he knew what he was going to do, there was no feeling about it. He was suspended, somehow, above the path that led through his pasture, uphill and to the woods in the hollow below his cotton field.

Two dollars and eleven cents, maybe. That's what he had lost by not catching the bus and going to his job; maybe more, depending on McIntosh's mood, since he had fired workers for not showing up. George wondered if McIntosh would think the shooting of Willie Jerdan, the fact that he had lain for more than an hour beside George's barn, would justify his not showing for work.

The ambulance and more officers had come sometime after daybreak. George deliberately avoided replaying their questions, warnings, the talk (although the gist of it, unspoken but clear, was that George by virtue of the fact that the dead man's girlfriend was even then inside George's house, and that Willie Jerdan had burrowed up in a pile of nubbins in George's crib, was somehow tied in with it, although they did not charge him or flat-out accuse him of harboring the escaped prisoner) but he knew he would nevertheless bear watching as far as they were concerned. Which meant he'd have to be doubly careful about seeing Paula.

But if she were home now, I would go. She won't know although she may hear. If I could only talk with her.

The children had not gone to school, and Nathan would have come with him now, but George wanted to be alone. After walking along the field's edge, George slid on pine straw, going downhill diagonally until he stood beside a dead sweet-gum tree. He put his jacket down, spit in his hands, gripped the handle and started swinging. Chips flew, chocolate brown gashes opened, then white.

He swung furiously, attacking the tree as though his life depended on it; hacking feverishly until bare branches began to shake, to move against limbs of other trees. Soon he had the trunk whittled in half. He dropped the ax and sat on the hillside. For he had heard a train's whistle and had, in his mind, also heard the other long lonely wail that had pierced his sleep and the quiet of the night.

Who is she? I do not even know Rosa's last name; but she knew, as soon as the shot sounded, or maybe before, she knew because she screamed. I heard her scream and I heard the shot. She has come into my house, into my life. Accidentally, I guess, like my moving here was an accident. If I had not been here, had not come around that barn at that precise moment, maybe she would have gone to the Gordons. Or maybe she would have had her baby on the railroad.

He heard the train again. It would be close now to the Quarters; it would be in the area of the bridge.

And if Willie had not been at that specific place (he was shot in the throat; I did not see that until daylight), who knows? He did not bleed much. Or maybe it was because he is black I could not see the blood. Against his skin. I didn't know him, but I feel hollow, and Rosa's crying does not seem real, but I will never forget it. Now, today, at this moment, none of it seems real.

The train passed. Even from where he sat, George felt the ground tremble and the whistle blowing for the crossing was loud, permeating the wooded hollow. He thought of the other crossing and of the Five & Dime Store down the hill from it, tried to visualize Paula at work.

He could not see Paula's face and felt detached, cold, thinking of her as the stranger she was in the beginning; cut off emotionally from her as wind blew cool against his skin. He wanted to call her back, to feel the warmth again, but at that moment he could not feel. And could not, in that unfeeling moment, believe he had held her, that she had turned her face to find him and he was empty, and something else was gone from him that she had given; something as untouchable as smoke—the way he had felt almost from the start with her—of being himself—of new value. He looked at his hands and thought: Who am I?

That person who had been in her house, held her, felt her love, who had smelled her perfume and kissed her was someone else, and those two unsatisfactory nights in her drafty bedroom were far away and not part of him. The him, George Malone, who sat on the hillside (chilled because he was sweaty) was not the him either who had on another day built his own house and plowed a double team of horses and was in control to the point of actually planning to own a cabinet-shop.

That man was not the one who had stood in the police station feeling guilty of something, ashamed, as he had felt in the sheriff's car and beside the dead Willie and afterwards, answering strangers' questions, not wanting to be afraid or ashamed or less than they, but feeling it anyway. I served on the grand jury. I was foreman. In Texas.

The face and the crumpled body of Willie came again— blue torso caught in the circle of light, short, small, lying there. The memory would not go away, nor would the cold way the officers had acted, the way they looked—or did not look—at Willie Jerdan.

They do not look. They do not see, not just the Colored. They do not see me either. He cut himself a chew of tobacco, carefully trimming a corner off the plug.

Under the memory, like the suspended tragedy of that early morning, was an unfocused image of Ox Hill. It was like a movie reel clicking backward, reversing: places they had been since the disastrous cotton crop failure at Horton; the swarm of unknown people who had been there; who were now there not as individuals but as a group, like a keg of ten-penny nails, only not like this either, not clean, strong, the way new nails seemed to him—more like rusted, bent, twisted, used, discarded nails; and somehow he, they, his family, Thelma, had gotten mixed with these, not to be looked at, even, any more. Separately.

She looks at me. She sees me. Yes.

Some of the strangeness he had just felt about Paula disappeared; tiny flecks of warmth swam again. And I see her. I know her. *She was a shiny ten-penny nail, apart from the others.* George remembered how he had felt like himself again because of her, because she had looked at him, and he had sensed a knowing in her and had felt known by her.

He lifted the ax, let the handle lean against his leg as he surveyed the beavered-out, unfinished gum. I felt better even before I ever touched her than I have since we left Texas.

He walked up the hill, along the edge of the field of dead stalks and brown claw-like bolls, to the railroad and, rather than take the path, he went on to the road. With her, he thought, I felt like a carpenter. It did not square overall in the house that was George Malone's life, but in the tiny room inside him where Paula lived, it squared.

The truck, parked about where the officers had been with their lights shining on the oak tree, belonged to Jim Sanders, George thought, and then knew because he saw him on the porch. Sanders, who had been about to knock, saw him, too, and met him on the path to the barn. He wore a leather jacket and gray whipcord breeches. One eye was afflicted, a milky chip in the otherwise amber circle.

"Howdy." His hand swallowed George's. The hand was bony, like his face.

"Trying to get in a little wood before it turns cold."

"Say, I wanted to tell you, I'm sure sorry about what happened here."

"It was a nightmare."

"Know it must have been. If I hadn't had some hauling to do, I'd been here sooner."

They walked to the place where Willie had been; George showed him.

"I knowed Willie, back when he was a boy and I was peddling. His daddy done some plowing for me before he got killed in the mines. Willie wasn't never a bad young'un." He fished out tobacco and papers and rolled a cigarette. "Reckon you might need some help getting the girl home."

"I could sure use some, yessir."

"I thought if it was transportation you need, we can use my old truck. They'll be having the funeral. Course, they'll mourn for a week, ten days. Figured she'd want to be home."

"I'd be much obliged," said George.

They stood where Willie Jerden died and, ten feet away was where Rosa had gone down at the start of her labor.

He fell and died ten feet away from where the first pain struck Rosa, George thought, where, you could say, a new life started. Within a week I saw a human life start and one end, and she screamed both times.

I don't know what either one means. Arthur Dee to grow up half white and half black. Will they look at him? Will they shoot him some day over a nickel or dime loaf of bread? Will he find a place for himself, if they don't shoot him?

"They ain't holding it agin you, George. I talked to her mama this morning—she buys vegetables from me summertime—

they appreciate what you've done. Any feelings won't be agin you. Lots of folks don't understand how the Coloreds are. They don't get involved with white folks' troubles. Stay to themselves."

"Maybe I did wrong."

"Nope. You done the right thing. And they know it."

In the house, George said, "Rosa, I know you want to go to Willie's funeral. Mister Sanders says he'll take you and Arthur Dee home. I'll ride up with you."

"I come back? I works good."

"I don't know," George said. "You got a baby to take care of first. And yourself." He wanted to say something about Tatum, but he didn't know how.

Rosa sat with knees straddling the gear shift. She held the baby, wrapped in the blanket George had bought the day that Sammy was born. Sanders hopped in, patted the accelerator and turned the switch. The truck backed, then shot forward, spun around and Sanders jerked it into second gear.

"You miss a day's work, George?"

"Yeah I did."

The truck was noisy and jerky. Rosa looked straight ahead. "Willie dead," she said. "My Willie gone."

On their right as they rode, there was the dead field of corn stalks standing crooked, a few straggling fronds blowing in the wind.

A loaf of bread, Malone thought.

#

# Chapter 19

On Friday evening after Thanksgiving they walked from the bus, hands clasped in the dark. This touching filled him with sureness. Quiet as they walked, but not an awkward quiet; they did not need to talk. He felt blood pulsing in their locked fingers.

They saw no one in the store's pale light, but he looked at her, her dark sparkling eyes and smoked-honey hair. Their shadows wavered ahead as they crossed the bridge. It had rained until late morning and now was cooler. Paula shivered as they turned off the road, toward her house.

She shivered later, too, when he felt her cream-smooth stomach, gently touched, and not even a thin line of light shone under the door.

He could barely see her face (pillowed beneath his); eyes so close he could see **them**, and her breath tip-toeing on his face. Paula Hogan, whose crushed-fruit lips were whispering, sounds surfacing. Paula with him there, actually held closely (round, burnished thigh small, lifting) face pressing, straining. Presence incredible. The soft strength of her thigh was yielding, her head near in close shadows.

Looking at her in darkness, he held off fast-rushing tide until **then**. Face quick-turned to muffle (against him) full hollow glass-enclosed "O!" Then dry sea whisper in his ear ("mister malone" . . .) as his own face settled in the feathery hair, and he lay with his arm around her.

She moved to the curve of his arm, head light on his shoulder as they faced the ceiling. Her voice was part of the dark, although he barely heard, did not need to hear. Did not need, either, to see, for he knew her.

Then she touched his eyes, temples. It was black, quiet, in the strange cold room.

"I tried to write to him last night. All I could think to tell about was you . . . I know! But I wanted to! Isn't that strange? But I want to tell *somebody*."

"I know. I wish I could, too. I wish I could tell about you."

"You can tell *me*."

"No." For how could he, what right had he, to say how he wanted to care for her always? To give, always to give, that's what he wanted.

". . . even when he kisses me. Not gentle, the way you are. It is like he is mad. And because I never say how I feel." She turned, kissing George's face. "I can tell you everything."

Yes, always to feel this. If I could know, have that. Her remembering. Even after Buzz Hogan comes home and whatever happens. If I could just *know*.

"All the times he's been away I never . . . but you . . . oh, George!"

Tenderness, but more—the ache in him in that second of not having her and of not being able to have her, knowing there was no bottom to it, and she—her life to come—was floating in darkness, untied so that he would not be able to talk with her at midnight, or see her when she awoke. Ever. He felt, with her, a hunger beyond desire (knowing she was married to Buzz Hogan), still wanting somehow a stake in her life. And to be there when she needed him, as she surely would, and to protect her from all the Tatums of the world. But she was floating, even now, away from him. He heard the whistle of the train passing under the bridge as he pushed back covers and moved away from her.

"Last night . . ." She reached for his hand. "He knocked."

"Who? You mean Tatum? Are you sure?"

"Yes. I turned off the light real fast, and I was quiet for a long time, but he said, 'Are you lonesome?' Then I heard the screen-door close and he walked off the porch."

# Chapter 20

It was awareness of loss more than guilt or depression, or perhaps all of these as he walked because she was floating beyond him, yet always in him (dark, glass-enclosed hurting night-cry to haunt), to quicken him forever.

Walking across the high, hollow sounding bridge toward familiar habitat, environment, life, culmination of bits and pieces of things that had happened, toward home. Homeward past the store, toward the road—going home.

And she and that place, that dark place where he had left her while wanting to comfort her in that hollow, sensitive afterwards, this place with her already far from him and beyond, so that he could feel the bottomless, empty fact of not being able to absorb her life into his, to protect and have, and give.

Still, he was a stranger hulled out of his body—new, renewed, strong, loved and wanted.

Transformed. Different from the helpless pawn whose very welfare job was about to play out. Somehow closer to how he once felt—but also fragile inside, wondering how she was feeling; filled with tender hurting loneliness. And fear. Remembering the closeness of her small body, George felt a hunger that would be forever unappeased.

But somewhere was the thought that maybe even so she had achieved a newness (despite her four years with the South

China Sea sailor). He held to this—her response. Maybe some way special to her. After all.

As he made his way through the cool night, toward the smoke-scented, drafty house that had become, through a series of job-seeking events, home, it was as though he himself were walking off the edge of the earth; a floorless feeling, worse because he had left her, and because he had left with her a vital part of himself.

What if she were to get pregnant? What would I do? I wish . . . that is part of how I feel. I would like to be with her and know my baby was growing in her. I don't want her to get pregnant Lord knows but the way I feel about her I mean it would be good to be her child's father, looking after them, seeing them together, seeing her nurse him. I can't take care of my own. I just wish I could be some part of her life . . .

It is when I think of losing her. She said always but . . . having to leave her is terrible. It is good for her to want, need me. And for me to know I am worth something, can feel. It does not seem wrong except not being able to be there. I think about her by herself. And about him, Tatum. It is worse now to think of these things. I did not set out to, but I know her. Mis-ter Malone . . . the way she said that.

Silver ball-bearings were scattered in the blue clear sky, and George saw moonlight across the front porch of his house. He stepped where it was shining on the planks, and compassion flooded him. He put a hand on one of the posts and looked at the stars, at the pink fluttering sky from the steel mills of Marbletown. The implausible realized closeness with Paula lay fragile inside him like a piece of glass. He felt lifted out of the drab uncaring WPA world; he was in touch with the bright sky even while he felt a loneliness and fear for the safety of her. Alone.

Voices from inside—already heard by Father/George— penetrated, the house focusing with children's voices. Turning to the door, George listened briefly to the quarreling voices, which were separated from him, which quieted, like wind suddenly stopped, as he opened the door.

"Thank the Lord you're home," said Thelma, standing in the kitchen door, "so you can put a stop to this infernal fussing. What? Miss the bus?"

"No. It was late."

"I got your supper warm, such as it is."

George flaked off burnt chips of peeling, revealing dark orange inside of a baked sweet potato, sliced butter from a round molded cake, split the deep golden potato and slid in the butter.

"What's wrong with the kids?"

"They've been fussing and fighting all blessed evening. Sammy mostly."

"Nathan started it," said Sammy. "Called me scaredy-cat."

"Well, you run off from Buddy Rickles. I wouldn't let nobody call me what he called Sammy and get away with it."

"Who's Buddy Rickles?"

"A big boy," said Sammy. "He's failed school two or three times."

"Sawed off like a rotten stump!" said Nathan.

"Ain't neither!"

George put his arm around Sammy, letting him hide his face against his shoulder.

"I don't want you kids fighting," he said, "if you can help it. But I don't want you being scared either. Go on, now. Do your school work."

I didn't use to be, George thought, for it came to him that he himself was scared; had been for a long time. How it had happened without his even knowing. Not Tatum as Tatum, but scared of Tatum all the same—of not being able to do anything about him, not able to get his pig back, or to protect her; scared of some unnamed thing. Scared of coming finally to the edge and not being able to find a job or feed his family.

This is what he hated most about Ox Hill, how everybody was scared of something. Even Higgins and his bunch, marching down to tell him he'd better get rid of Rosa. Scared. Scared, maybe, of the thing that had them all hemmed in. He had seen it, too, in the faces of the Coloreds.

She is not like that. Of course she is afraid, like when he (Tatum) knocked, but not scared the way the rest of us are. With her I am not scared either. *Except*

"What are you going to do?" asked his wife. "About a job."

He drained the milk from his glass. "I don't know. What do you want me to do?"

"I just asked."

"Go into the mines, I guess. Jim Sanders says I probably can get on. He knows somebody." He saw her face tighten.

"Now wouldn't that be nice! And you with five kids depending on you. Go down there and get yourself killed!"

"It's work."

"Well, I had hoped maybe . . ."

"What? Hoped what?"

"That you could find something somewhere else . . ."

"There ain't somewhere else! I can't stand another move. Besides, where?"

"I don't know," Thelma snapped. "It's your place to . . ."

"Yes, it's my place." He didn't want to argue. He understood that what he said did not matter to her—really did not matter as it once had. "I told Sanders to do what he could."

"You used to call yourself a carpenter."

George pushed away from the table and walked to the window. "Well, I don't call myself nothing any more. Nothing but a scared jack-rabbit, trying to stay one jump ahead."

He looked into the night. The good part had gone. Only guilt now.

"I never wanted to go into the mines," he said quietly, seeing his wife's face reflected in the window. "But show me a choice. Maybe then we could get a doctor without going halfway around the world."

He turned, head cocked. "What was that?"

"Daddy," Willa Marie called. "Somebody's at the door."

At first he thought it was a dog on the porch beyond the screen, but when he heard "Mistah Malone, Mama say—" his eyes focused, picked dark out of darkness, although he didn't know yet who the boy was or, until he opened the screen, that he was Colored.

Then he did know that it was the kid he had seen astride a bicycle on the bridge, asking "Is you got a quatah?," but not knowing enough, so that he instinctively went out on the porch and closed the door. Knowing also—feeling his stomach squeeze, contract around nothing—that whatever the boy was trying to say concerned Paula. George stooped and asked, "What is it, Son? What's wrong?"

"Mama say you bettah come about that white lady. She hut."

The sky broke as though the world had shifted, as though the flicker from the Marbletown mills might be approaching as a wall of flame, which was already devouring the world.

George grabbed, feeling thin shoulder-bone in his tight grasp, leaning closer, whispering: "What happened to her? Tell me!"

"She hut."

"What you mean, she's hurt? What is it?"

"Mama say . . ."

"Where is she?" Aware then that the shoulder was pulling away; large eyes clearly stretched wide, everything clear now in the no-longer total blackness, and George turned loose.

"She at Mama's." The boy moved, was shorter because he had jumped off the porch and was lifting the bicycle.

"Wait. I'll go with you. Wait now."

He was inside, still unable to sort it out, but moving.

"What's wrong?"

"Trouble at the Quarters. Rosa's mammy sent the boy."

"Surely to goodness you're not going! What kinda trouble? How come they send for you ever blessed time trouble pops up? You can't go out in the middle of the night . . ."

"I got to."

"You ain't even got your coat."

"Get it." His eyes focused on Willa Marie. "Find my coat."

"You're liable to get yourself killed, messing with a buncha drunk nig . . ."

"Y'all go to bed!"

The boy was in the road. George saw the outline of wheels against light.

"If that don't beat all," he heard Thelma say, as his foot hit the ground.

\#

# Chapter 21

Where a fat black woman had lain on that Sunday morning, now Paula, with swollen purplish cheekbone, honey hair against faded sofa. She lay in sixty-watt shadows, eyes containing all the secret knowing between them, confirming instantly that George need no longer lie in fear of its happening because it had already happened and was over. And would never be over.

Not Rosa, holding her pink baby, or her mother, or the children were what he saw, but the eyes, after the eternal time it took to get there, after his hand touched the cold metal of rusty gate and then the door. The eyes. He knelt on the rag-rug and held her tightly, listening to quiet sobbing.

Tight circle of room holding tighter circle of them, so that the woman's saying: "Mistah Malone, I thought you mought ought to know. I thought *he* want to know . . ." did not register. Only she, clinging, tears staining both their faces, existed. He kissed the purple puff that had replaced the soft cheek.

"I thought it was you," she whispered. "I thought you had come back!"

Arthur Dee cried then, but George did not hear or care that it was the same voice that had first sounded in his house, and did not see black breast exposed by Rosa, two feet away, holding the same baby whose birth had brought him joy.

"Y'all go in yonder. Raymond, you chilren, shoo now. Git.

Rosa, take your baby chile somewhere."

Tatum's dirty hands, thought George; only not thought, articulated, but feeling, partially hidden, still far enough away for him to not know fully; it was working its way into his brain: His dirty hands had touched her.

"I heard somebody crying, fumbling wit the gate and Rosa said, 'It the white lady,' and I done what I could, Mistah Malone, and I say to Raymond, I say 'You go tell Mistah Malone.'"

"I didn't want her to send . . ."

"She tell the truth. She sho tell the truth. She say for me not to, but I thought . . ."

"I'll get a doctor." He said it calmly. The real hurt was still coming into focus.

"No! No, no no."

"Baby, I have to . . ."

"You can't. Don't you see?"

"I done what I could for her. Like I done for Rosa . . ."

"We've got to get a doctor."

"I just done what I knows to do, that's all . . ."

"I thought it was you. It was just after you left. Oh, I wanted it to be you. I opened the door. I opened . . . and he . . ."

George held her. "Shhh, now. Shhh."

"He a bad bad man. Mmm-mmm!" Her shadow fell across them. "Co'se, Mistah Malone, you knows was we to call the law, they would say one of our Colored mens do it."

"I know who did it!"

"Yassuh, co'se you does. We all knows. But was we to call the law . . ."

"All I could remember was that you said Rosa lived here . . ."

"And you walked over here? Sweet Paula, I'm so sorry. It's my fault." *oh god yes I caused it . . . made her vulnerable*

George could see her, hurt, used and discarded by the hulking, grinning, stinking Tatum, stumbling alone through darkness to this house for help. Then, only then, he thought of his shotgun, which should have been the first thing he thought of.

"You got Willie's gun?"

The woman didn't answer, and Paula clutched him.

"Say? I want Willie's pistol!"

"Lawdy mercy!" She didn't look at him; her lips pouted; her head swayed. "Lawd hep us."

"Get the gun," George ordered. "You hear?"

"Ain't got no gun, don't believe."

Paula tugged at his sleeve. "Please hold me. Don't go over there . . ."

"I goes look, but I pretty sure I ain't got no pia-stol. I ask Rosa but I pretty sure . . ." She turned before drawing the curtain that separated the rooms. "Mistah Malone, I don't think you needs no pia-stol."

George was shaking.

"You just get yourself in trouble for that no-good white man. You don't need . . ."

"Get it!"

"Don't. Please don't. Please just stay with me. Hold me."

"I'll kill him." He paced the floor, whirled. "He . . ." His voice broke. "I knew. I knew . . ."

"I don't find no pia-stol. I done looked . . ."

George jerked the door. The knob fell, rolled, and as he rushed off the porch, he heard Paula: "Come back!" and the woman, following, saying "Lawd hep us . . ."

Going into blackness, face tingling, throat constricted, George was running even before he got the gate open, tripping slightly as he took the high step out of the yard, rushing, choked with fury as the cold night air stung him. Her house, jagged limb-shadows accenting its aloneness, fed his pain, so there was no room to plan or think how he would do what he would do. Then he was on Tatum's porch, kicking the screenless door. It splintered, and he was inside, yelling, "Where are you, you sonofabitch?"

Shapes materialized in the dark, voices sleepy, frightened, arose in the thick blackness, but he saw, in the narrow front room, a lighter mass moving, rising, from a bed. Then his hands were pulling, and he smelled Tatum: unwashed, filthy in long underwear—but he held, caught, finally, a kicking leg while a scream from the bed verified what he had wondered, that yes, the man had a wife.

A foot landed in George's face but he held, pulling until the mass loosened, slid, fell thumping to the floor. He dragged Tatum, backing toward the door, stumbling, weaving with the threshing legs, until he was on the porch. Tatum came off the floor, crouching, and George shoved him into the yard, got his hands on the massive throat and squeezed. He rode the threshing body, holding, lifting, trying to pound the head into the ground, while voices came from the house.

Movement on the porch and someone, a child, put hands on his shoulders; then a broom struck his head so that he loosened his grip, half-turning to see the attacking woman. Tatum lunged, got a free upward swing, knocked George off, threw himself against George's legs as he struggled to stand.

George fell flat, and the back of his head smacked the ground. The spinning inside his head slowed his reflexes, so that he lay, unable to get up but saw Tatum coming with the double-bit ax.

Seeing the arms go up, George fought to come out of his stupor, heard a roar, and was aware of a flash of fire somewhere; knew Tatum was standing but had never completed the swing. He waited for Tatum to fall, but instead a voice, Colored voice, words: "Leave Mistah Malone . . . let him be . . ."

Then five, six, maybe more, dark figures moved in. George got to his knees, saw the ax against the ground although the handle was still in Tatum's hand—and the moving figures surrounded them.

"You don't hut Mistah Malone," a voice close was saying as George got to his feet. There were more than six; others were moving in from the road.

The woman on the porch: "He's trying to kill my man!" And Tatum was saying something, cursing, saying " . . . damn niggers . . ." and the man with the gun stuck the end of the barrel against Tatum's stomach and the voice said, "Shut yo' mouth."

Another man stepped toward Tatum. He looked at George and raised his hand: a blade catching a glint of moonlight. "What you say about it? We do what *you* say."

From the porch: "Daddy!"

George, aware now of warm blood dripping from his face and tasting his bleeding tongue, stared at Tatum, heard the high-pitched whine: "Don't let 'em hurt me, hear? You can have your pig . . ."

George swiped at the blood on his face, his head spinning. He looked into the face of the man with the knife, saw the lips move. He smelled whisky. He looked at the circle of men.

"No," he said. "No."

George heard mumbles as he turned from Tatum, away from the narrow house, away from the sagging porch with the woman and whimpering kids.

"No," he repeated.

He began to speak to the man standing near him, but his legs gave away, and he could not clearly see him. And then he could see nothing, but he felt it when his body hit the ground.

* * *

He saw the stars and felt cold air on his face—someone was holding his legs, his arms, his body was hanging free between, moving. Someone was behind, trying to steady his bobbling head. Then they stopped, and a voice said: "Come on, Junior. Come around and open the gate. This man be bleeding."

And: "Yes'm, he gonna be awright."

#

# Chapter 22

Strangers, all, sitting on the worn wooden curved-back benches as George burst into the depot, tiny drops of rain sticking to his mackinaw. But he did not see her.

A pudgy hand held a newspaper in front of him. "Wanta buy a paper?"

No. I only want to find her. Please don't be gone.

Quickly he walked across the hard tile floor under the oval, colored-glass, high and hollow depot ceiling. Voices droned like bees in a drum, but he was alone.

Then he saw her, next to the wall not ten feet away, holding a bottle of red soda pop. Neat, small inside the tan coat with furred collar, she came to him.

Sweet cold strawberry taste.

He felt her sag against him so that without his arms she would have fallen. It was theirs—this stopped unticking minute that answered everything. They did not speak until after they had walked to the benches.

"I can't believe you're actually here. How did you know?"

"McIntosh sent us home, said 'You can't put a roof on in this rain,' and I went to see you. She told me."

"You were going to kill him! Or get killed. Because of me." She touched where there was a swelling below one eye. "When they brought you in, I thought he had killed you."

"He almost had."

George was silent, then. He did not say what he had practiced saying. There was nothing to be argued. She held a piece of paper that said 1:58 p.m., which would finish it, take her away, take away the special now-bruised her with whom he had lain in that back room. But never fully. Dream-like *her* whose very her-ness would cry out to him always, kindling desire and wish to protect, share, hold against all the cruelty that had burst in, after all, had come through the very door that he himself had opened.

"You are the kindest man . . ." she whispered. Her eyes were full of tears.

George looked at her face—planed smooth, rich deep-skinned cream—and at the delicate little mouth that he knew was neither little nor delicate nor timid nor prim nor scared; feeling again how it was that first day when she had turned to him—the exact second when he had known that her mouth would touch his with an intimacy that had opened the way for knowing her.

"I feel safe when I'm with you." Her fingers pulsed strong against his.

Black hands on the giant clock, so high it could not be touched without a ladder, told silently that in less than thirty minutes she would be gone.

"That's what started it, Paula—wanting you to be safe. That's what it was from the start." And look at what happened, what I caused—let—happen. The yellowish-purple spot on her face was only partially hidden by makeup.

I done for her like I done for Rosa. Only Rosa had his baby anyway.

If it happened . . . if . . . She would not know whether it was his or mine! And I won't know anything. Something broke inside him so that he suddenly missed whatever had been there. He looked at the tiny scar beside her mouth and at her eyes, at all of her, close, softly beautiful in the dimness. "You ought to have seen a doctor."

"I couldn't. You would have been mixed up in it. Besides, Buzz must never know." She touched his arm. "I wanted *you* to know."

I really won't know anything from here on. Or see you. Or be any part of you or even know where you are, and all I have felt will be left back there. Already is left.

Trains, coming and going, and people together briefly before scattering but I thought I would know forever have in some way always

"If you knew how I feel . . ."

"I do."

You will never understand exactly, and in a little while it will not matter to you, or maybe you will hate me because of what I caused to happen. (And I will not know and all I ever will have is what I have had, briefly.)

"If they had not been there, he would have killed me with that ax. I don't even know who saved my life."

"They know you."

"They would've killed him for me. If I'd said to." *my choice*

"Rosa and her mother talked about you. They were so good to me."

"They knew about us all along, I guess."

"I know. I thought of that, that night."

"They all knew about us. Funny . . . that in the beginning I was afraid for you because of *them*."

The man with newspapers passed, waved the Birmingham News, stared.

"I do know them," George said. "The way I told you about Rosa's baby when I first saw him. Like that, I know them. Different from the others although I know the others, too, more than I thought." I know Tatum, too. Even him: And in that moment of knowing could not say yes when the man with the knife asked.

Paula checked her face in a small compact-mirror, touched powder to the bruised cheek, put the compact away.

George turned his face from her. He could not hold her any more than he could hold anything else. And because he was afraid of what might happen if he did not say something, he said, "This afternoon I'm going to Blackwater. To see Mister J.C. Culpepper who is the one that decides who can dig coal and who can't."

Paula clutched his hand, unfolded and caressed the strong limber fingers. "I want your hands to work with wood. Not dig coal."

"It's not like that, though."

"You're a carpenter," she whispered.

"A miner is a man, too. It doesn't make any difference, not as much as I once thought."

"You're different. A lot different."

"It was good to think so. I never pictured myself working in the mines. But plenty of folks have, and I don't guess they planned it that way, either."

"But you **are** different."

"Everybody is," said George. "But it is not just because of having a cabinet-shop or a bag full of pills. There's more to it."

He shivered as they stepped outside. The wind was blowing, and the olive coaches were waiting. People were boarding. Steam hissed up and down the track. They stopped near a baggage cart. He wiped lightly below her eyes, where a trace of tears lingered. The line of passengers was being swallowed quickly.

He held her tightly. But he could not hold her either. He had nothing to do with it now. He found her ear, nuzzled his way through the soft hair, whispered something.

He felt her lips, feverish in the cold dampness. She said softly, "Mister Malone" and smiled.

Then she was gone, her heels clicking the few feet across the concrete platform. She stepped quickly into the train.

George saw her smoked-honey hair blowing slightly as she disappeared.

The train jolted, jerked, and he heard it squeaking and bumping all up and down the line. A scrap of newspaper fluttered across the platform.

#

# Chapter 23

Black hands folded white butcher-paper around the chunk of cheese. Doing this against the greasy counter top between glass cases holding pig's feet, bacon, fatback, spare-ribs.

She dropped the package into a sack, which already contained meal and flour, baking soda, kitchen-matches, Octagon soap, lollipops for the kids.

She reached for a plug of tobacco, which he had laid on the counter, but George said, "You needn't put that in the sack. I'll take it."

"Yassuh, I 'spect you gonna try that 'fore you gets home." He saw a flash of gold beyond the smile.

"Yes'm." He looked around the high-ceiling, dingy store: shadowy shelves of canned food, work gloves, Irish potatoes in a bin, red apples.

"Something else?"

"No, I guess not." He started to pay her, then remembered, or thought of what he was looking for. Or something that might in some small way substitute for what he was looking for. "You got any strawberry pop?"

metal box with flaking red Coca-Cola and a smiling girl in a straw hat holding a moisture-beaded bottle

Which would be more appetizing in July than now, the third day of January.

"Sody pop? I reckon maybe there is some strawerberry."

"I can get it," he said, seeing her start around the counter.

He lifted a cold, wet bottle from the box, snapped off the cap and took a swallow of the too-sweet drink. He gave her the money.

"How long you reckon 'fore the snow gonna melt?" An amber comb was stuck in her steel-wool hair.

He saw again the gold in her mouth as she made the little bell ring on her ancient register. She dropped change into his waiting hand.

"Two, three days yet, I expect. Unless it rains."

"Yassuh. Well, it slipped up on me yestiddy when I wakes up and see the ground all white."

"It's pretty," George said.

"Yassuh, cept'n when it comes to getting out in it. You oughter warm yourself by the stove 'fore you goes back out."

"This is all right," said George.

He moved to stand beside one of the shelves, facing the outdoors, while he drank the red pop. It did not taste good, though. It did not help.

"Thank you, Mistah Malone."

"You're welcome, Lady."

He pulled the brim of his gray hat lower and, holding the sack in the crook of his arm, went out. Two inches of snow, already streaked yellow, lay on the ground in front of the store. George felt cold bite his face and hands and slice inside his nostrils.

He turned left and walked to the bridge over the railroad tracks. It was colder there, out in the open space.

Wind, without the black load that burdens the trains, swept quickly and silently between the banks, along the tracks, and lashed him as he stood on the bridge. Snow powdered the banister, light, icy, and he brushed off some and watched its long scattered fall.

He set the groceries beside him and fished the tobacco from his jacket. He slit the cellophane wrapper with his knife and cut a corner off the light-brown cake. Below and down the tracks, he could see black lumps of coal partially covered with white.

Tomorrow. Tomorrow would be soon enough to think of that.

He scooped a handful of snow off the banister, squeezed it into a cold lump, held it. Cars had packed the snow against the creosoted crossties that floored the bridge.

Wind blew tiny sprays of powder off the caked snow, blew into the streaks left by his hand on the banister.

Slow wind-blown voices (which he had actually heard on a Sunday morning from the wooden church where the Coloreds sang) singing, saying I am bound for the pra-ham-ised land halle-lu-jah

He could hear, too, the click on other days against the floor of the bridge.

That moment that exact moment when her face reached for mine, turned, so that I knew. That first second when I touched her lips, I knew her. *what a price we pay for knowing*

He threw the snowball over the bridge and watched its icy shatter.

Tomorrow he would ride one of the little cars down into the ground at Blackwater.

Tomorrow, for the first time in his life, he would get on his knees and pick coal free of the underground vein. But he did not think of explosions or falling rocks, or feel fear, which could trip the blackness inside his own veins.

Instead he thought of her lips and heard again as though coming across a hot dry field at noon: mister malone.

**-Finis-**

CPSIA information can be obtained at www.ICGtesting.com
Printed in the USA
LVOW080426231012

303996LV00001B/1/P